MERMAID OF NEW YORK

MERMAID OF VENICE: BOOK THREE

JINCEY LUMPKIN

ABOUT THE AUTHOR

JINCEY LUMPKIN is a writer who splits her time between NYC and Lisbon. She has been profiled by Dateline NBC, *Vice*, and *GQ*, among others. *Out* Magazine listed her in its "OUT 100", naming her as one of the world's most influential LGBTQ+ people, alongside celebrities like Laverne Cox and Ricky Martin.

Scan the QR code below to join my email newsletter or visit Jincey-Lumpkin.com/Front-Matter

SCAN ME

facebook.com/jinceylumpkin

twitter.com/jinceylumpkin

instagram.com/storiesbyjincey

Names, characters, businesses, places, events, locales, and incidents are either the products of the author's imagination or used in a fictitious manner. Any resemblance to actual persons, living or dead, or actual events is purely coincidental.

Ebook: 978-1-7364712-5-8
Print: 978-1-7376155-4-5
Hardcover: 978-1-7376155-5-2

CIP Block/Library of Congress Number:
1-10686057161

First edition January 2022.

Edited by Amanda E. Clark
Cover art by Jason Brooks
Cover art direction by Matthew Axe
Cover layout by Lauren Balistreri

To my little brother, Chad, with much love and affection. I remain ever grateful for your support and equally as awed by all you have accomplished. I know in my heart that we're making our parents very proud.

Wake up bud,
hit the light.
See the old man
in a polecat fight.

ACKNOWLEDGMENTS

I want to thank my office buddies, Sujal, Dave, Gerald, Schidlow, Mumu, and Khari for encouraging and inspiring me to seek creative fulfilment outside the practice of law. Your support sent me on a twisty, satisfying path. And shoutout to our office sisters, Rose and Zenobia, for putting up hours and hours of our annoying shenanigans.

Thank you to my editor, Amanda. In the process bringing these three books to life, we've built both a professional and a personal relationship. I look forward to nurturing our new friendship and eagerly await the many adventures I imagine we will have together. Also, please finish your own novel.

Many thanks to Matthew Axe, Jason Brooks, and Lauren Balistreri for your immense talent and for continuing to make these books look so stunning on the shelf.

Thank you to my readers for coming back, book after book. I adore you. Without you, these worlds would exist only in my mind.

Lastly, as always, my love and gratitude goes out to my wife Eva. You love me even on my worst days. You give me the wingspan to fly as high as I might dare. Darling, love of my life, we will both accomplish incredible feats. I believe in you as much or more than I believe in myself.

TRIGGER WARNING

This book contains intense descriptions of graphic sex, violence, and abuse, including emotional abuse, murder and torture.

1

September 15th

Gia was exhausted after the car ride from Portugal. Her security team exited the vehicle to sweep the rural airport outside Paris, near Rouen. There was another plane in the hangar, along with its owner and pilot, but no press and no one with cameras. Fame was not Gia's forte, and as her notoriety had increased, so had her paranoia.

Her phone rang, and she answered it as she stepped out of the SUV. It was her real estate broker, Abby Singer, calling.

"I've found the perfect New York apartment for you." Known as the Queen of Celebrity Deals in Manhattan, rumors had swirled around Abby, and there had been speculation that she'd been the one to smuggle Katie Holmes into NYC during her seemingly overnight split from Tom Cruise. But Abby's lips were sealed on that matter.

"*Finalmente,*" Gia said, "tell me more."

Abby spoke rapidly, and it took quite a lot of effort for Gia to keep up with her. "It's a pre-war on Park Ave, steps from the park. Classic layout with four beds, five baths, doorman, huge fireplace. Stunning. The crown molding is *to die*."

"Park Avenue? Four bedrooms? No. I told you six bedrooms at a minimum. I need a room for my daughter and space for my security staff. I do not care what the price is. Find me the biggest, safest apartment in Manhattan."

Gia hung up and slipped the phone in her bag, pulling her hat lower on her head.

As Gia waited to board her plane, her thoughts were occupied with her journey to New York—and her ensuing custody battle for Serena. Gia didn't notice that the other plane inside the hangar bore a familiar name: Bisset. Bisset Industries to be specific.

It wasn't until she saw a face from the past descending the airsteps of the other plane that she snapped out of her rumination.

"*Bonjour*, Gia," the man said.

"Florent, is that you?" Shocked, Gia's mouth dropped open.

Her security guards closed in around her, forming a protective circle, but she gave them the signal to back off.

"Gia," Florent winked, "you have not aged a day." He lightly tugged on the neck of his cashmere turtleneck to let in a bit of fresh air. It was much too early to wear any kind of sweater, let alone cashmere, but Florent had his reasons for the choice of wardrobe—and they had nothing to do with fashion.

Gia was dumbfounded, confused. She never thought she'd see him again—much less witness him stepping off of a jet emblazoned with his last name.

As he edged closer to her, she took a step backward. "It's all right," he cooed. "I heard about everything that happened to you in Sicily. I am just happy that I was able to help you."

"*Help* me?" Gia shook her head, trying to process everything. "I do not understand. What do you mean?"

"We share a common friend... Awa Diop."

"Awa? How do you know Awa? I am sorry, but this is all coming as quite a shock to me."

On the other side of the hangar, Gia's pilot radioed to the flight attendant that the jet was ready to depart for Teterboro airport. The flight attendant then approached Gia's security team to begin boarding protocol. The head of security murmured into an earpiece, relaying that Gia would be ready to board the plane shortly.

Florent continued speaking. "Awa asked me to help coordinate smuggling you out of that psychopath's compound."

"*Why* would you do that?" Gia demanded.

"We are old friends, aren't we?" Florent's eyes narrowed, and inside them, Gia could see her own reflection. The corners of her mouth turned down.

"I do not think that we are." She felt tingling in her chest and a gnawing sense of anxiety. "I... I left you in St. Moritz."

"Indeed, you did. You left me in the snow all alone." He approached her, leaning close to her ear, whispering to her. "But I *lived*." He yanked his turtleneck down, revealing a thick diagonal scar that ran from the bottom left of his chin to his right shoulder. "You tried to kill me, Gia, but I lived."

2

July 23rd

"Thank God she has legs," Royce murmured while standing over his granddaughter's bassinet.

"For crying out loud, Royce," Bronwyn snapped, "stop saying that! I'm sick of hearing it."

He crossed his arms. "You can't tell me you're not happy she doesn't have a tail!"

"Don't listen to him, Serena," Bronwyn wrinkled her nose as she spoke to the newborn. "Grandmother Brownie would love you if you had five eyes. Isn't that right?"

Royce winced and walked backwards out of the room.

Bronwyn picked up the baby and eased into a gliding chair, rocking her. "Such a mean grand-daddy, isn't he? Well, nevermind that little one. You're the best baby in the whole world." Bronwyn picked up a walkie-talkie and radioed to the kitchen. "Bring in the milk, please."

Bronwyn held little Serena on her chest and glanced around the room. It had been Cameron's when he was a boy. On the side table was a photo of her son in his lacrosse uniform from his prep school days. Bronwyn's throat clenched up, and she turned her head and squeezed her eyes tight to hold the pain in place. She often felt that her grief might strangle the life out of her. At least she had her grand-baby now. Serena was a real comfort.

A young woman with a Roman nose slipped into the bedroom. "You want milk?" she asked, in a halting Russian accent.

"Yes, I think the baby is hungry."

"You go?" the woman asked, visibly uncomfortable.

"No, dear... I *stay*."

The woman unbuttoned her shirt and unhooked her nursing bra. Her plump breasts, round and full, toppled out. Her right breast was already leaking, so indeed, it was feeding time. The woman bent down over Bronwyn to pick up the baby. A few drops of her breast milk dripped on Bronwyn's shoulder.

"Be more careful, girl! This jacket is Chanel!" Bronwyn reached for a tissue, and dabbed it against the splatter. "Ugh, *Russians*," she muttered. "We should have paid extra for the American wet nurse. I will rectify this first thing in the morning."

Glaring at the woman breastfeeding Serena, Bronwyn rose and trudged over to the changing table to straighten a stack of diapers.

3

July 26th

It was an unusually warm day off the coast of Portugal. A grey catamaran bobbed in the Atlantic current. Emblazoned on the stern was a name: *Jaws*.

While the boat perhaps did not quite meet the qualifications to merit superyacht status, it was, nonetheless, impressively large. Per Gia's specific instructions, the vessel was anchored far enough away from Cascais that it did not draw the attention of vacationers on the Portuguese Riviera.

Inside, Gia paced the stateroom. Her breasts ached, cramping with excess milk. No baby, no mouth to feed. She felt entirely unhinged and out of control. A walking Greek tragedy.

What kind of person abandons a newborn? She berated herself, angry that her need for self-preservation had trumped her maternal instincts—mere moments after giving birth. *I should not have gone through with having this baby. This was a mistake. I am not a family-oriented person. How could I think that a child would ever be safe with me?*

Her thoughts, as they had many times before, turned to Cameron.

Maybe if he were alive, and we were together... perhaps in those circumstances I could have been a good mother. Maybe Serena is better off being raised by her grandparents?

The sputtering of an approaching motorboat interrupted her intrusive thoughts. She peeked out the porthole to see the First Mate skipping through the waves. Holding onto the edge of the boat for dear life was *La Nonna*.

The dinghy pulled up to the steps on the back of the boat, and a member of Gia's security team helped *La Nonna* on board.

"*Madonna!*" *La Nonna* cried, gripping her purse and swaying on the boat deck. "The waves... too much." She was positively green.

Gia waved *La Nonna* inside. "Come sit and have some water... and a dramamine."

La Nonna fell into an armchair and rested her head in her palms. A crewmember brought her a glass and a pill, which she reluctantly swallowed. "*Allora*," she whispered, trying to gather her thoughts. "Where would you like to begin?"

Gia launched into a series of questions. "What is happening with Serena? Have you heard anything about the Langleys? Is my baby all right?"

"As I told you on the phone yesterday, your baby is safe. The grandparents have taken her to their compound in New York."

"I imagined so," Gia sighed. "But how were they allowed to travel out of Italy with her? I thought such a thing was not permitted."

"It is not difficult when people have money and private planes, Gia. You know this. There is no guard posted at every tiny airport on the lookout for baby snatchers. Truly, you cannot be so naive."

Gia snapped her head in the older woman's direction, "I ask about the safety of my child, and you insult me? How dare you."

"I understand, I do. I am a mother, you know. I have already begun the Hague proceedings for custody."

"How long will that take?"

La Nonna shook her head and tossed up her hands. "Normally not more than six weeks or so... but *angioletta*, you are not a typical case. I am doing all that I am able in order to untangle you from your arrest warrant in Italy. And the Langleys have retained Edward Ford Huntington to argue their case."

"Who?"

"He is, without a doubt, the best family lawyer in Manhattan... perhaps the best one in all of the States. He is very well respected and extraordinarily connected. The cloud of suspicion around you... the murder of Nico... that will most certainly be used as a justification for allowing temporary... if not permanent... custody."

Gia blankly stared at her lawyer.

"I am doing my best, Gia. I assure you."

"Can we not just send someone to New York to take Serena from the house? Slip in and remove her while everyone is sleeping?"

La Nonna clicked her teeth, "These people, Gia... they have highly-trained security working for them... ex-military. I do not mean soldiers, *bella*. These men are former generals, arms dealers, ex-CIA... they have an electric fence of support, the voltage of which they have increased rather significantly since the murder of their son. How do you think they were able to kidnap *Signor* Mosca? If they have the power to effectively decapitate one of the heads of *Cosa Nostra*, what do you think they will do to you? Even if you take Serena from them, I doubt that they will allow you to keep her."

"But we could stay in Senegal... the colony there will allow me to live as a refugee... I am sure of it."

"And will you be happy trapped underwater like that? Not able to come ashore? I think not."

Gia frowned because *La Nonna* was right. She wouldn't last more than a month under the sea.

La Nonna continued. "No, the best way forward is to allow this to play out in the open. We must plead our case in public and let the gavel of justice land in our favor."

"And if it does *not* land in our favor?"

"Let us eat that cannoli when it has been fried, no? Perhaps we should turn our attention to your business affairs."

"Go on."

"*Bene, allora*... first, a new phone for you." *La Nonna* fished a flip phone out of her bag. "New technology, untraceable."

"How?"

"Gia, I do not make the phones, *angioletta*. I only pass them out. My technician worked for Moussad. If he says this is undetectable, then you could stand in the Vatican and order a bomb to be dropped on the Pope's little white hat without registering a warning signal. Understand? Do not lose this. It is the only one I have left."

Gia took the phone and held it in her sweaty palm.

La Nonna leaned back in the armchair and closed her eyes. The dramamine was taking effect, and she finally felt less nauseated. "I have sent instructions to Queen Awa and Moussa. They shall meet you here in four days to discuss the running of your company."

"And Vittore?"

"He is in Santorini with Uncle Stavros."

"Please send word to him that I am all right."

"I have already done so."

"At least Vittore is finding some happiness." Gia's lips spread into a half-smile, and her spirits lifted slightly.

"Apparently those old men are considering a wedding, but they want to wait for your return."

"A wedding!" Gia was beaming now. "Tell Vittore not to wait one single day. When I am able, I will throw him the biggest celebration the world has ever seen."

4

July 27th

Bronwyn rolled the stroller into her cottage. Serena, her sweet angel grandbaby, was fast asleep. Bronwyn steered carefully around the furniture and into the kitchenette, removing a bottle of Pinot from the wine fridge.

"Let's pour a big glass of Grandmother Brownie's magic grape juice." The wine glug-glugged nearly to the rim before Bronwyn shoved the cork back in and gulped down a big sip. Babies were exhausting. She didn't remember it being this hard with Cam and Harper. Then again, that was thirty-something years ago, and she had lots of help. Not that she couldn't afford nannies... she just wanted to be more hands-on with Serena.

Bronwyn slipped her index finger under one of Serena's golden curls and gently twisted it around. "My sweet darling. I love you so very much." Her heart twinged, and she withdrew her hand from the carriage. She cast her eyes over to the small urn that housed the part of Cameron's ashes that had not been interred.

She took another sip from her wine and pushed the baby over to the sofa, flipping on the wall of TVs and muting all but one. That television was tuned into a competitor network, LION, and on screen was Harper. Even if Bronwyn was still furious with her daughter about crossing the Rubicon and leaving OTN, part of her felt very proud to see Harper sitting on the throne of primetime—a feat possible due only to Harper's tenacity and shrewd strategies. Harper, her youngest child, was all grown up now.

She looked down at Serena and baby-talked to her, "Now, don't you go flying the coop, little one."

Fly the coop? Bronwyn thought. *That's the wrong way of saying it. Wouldn't it be "swimming upstream"... or something like? Banish the thought!*

On her TV screen, the studio lights brightened, and the camera focused on Harper.

"I come to you with breaking news this evening," Harper said. "Mermaid Gia Acquaviva is once again in the spotlight. The Italian arrest warrant in conjunction with the murder of Nicolás Ángel Fernández has been discharged. In a public statement, the authorities in Venice are citing a lack of evidence as the reason for this dismissal."

"Son of a bitch!" Bronwyn screamed reflexively and spilled some wine on her lap. Automatically, Serena awakened and began crying. Brownyn let out a frustrated sigh and reached down into the bassinet. She lifted Serena from underneath the soft cotton blankets.

What she saw shocked her—although it shouldn't have.

A tail, sparkling like a freshly-minted gold bar, swayed in the air. Nearly dropping Serena, Bronwyn placed the child back into her bassinet and grabbed the telephone.

"Royce," she said, voice shaky, "get in here right now! The baby's turned mermaid!"

"Oh, good Lord! No, no, no. Is she going to *stay* like that?"

"How would I know, for Christ's sake? Call the pediatrician and then come here immediately!"

5

May 1995

Florent spied an eerie gargoyle perched at the base of one of the cathedral's buttresses. Construction on the cathedral in his father's hometown had begun in the 12th century, and it took the townsfolk seven hundred years to complete. Florent had never noticed before, but the stone tympanium over the entrance to the nave featured a scene from the Bible depicting a lesser-known story about Samson's defeat of the Philistines and their god, Dagon, a merman.

C'est typique, Florent thought. *A merman? Harbor towns and fishermen are always so pedestrian.*

He had no idea what a coincidence it actually was that a mermaid floated above the door to where his father's closed-casket funeral was taking place.

Florent's mother, Sophie, took her son's hand as they entered the church. Sophie had been distraught since Pierre's death. Florent couldn't explain to his mother why his father had been up on the ledge of the apartment building—at least not without also telling her that he'd had an affair with his father's two lovers. So, he'd kept the truth to himself, and let his mother—and everyone else for that matter—believe that his father committed suicide.

As for Gia, he hadn't seen her since the police and *pompiers* scraped his father's body off Avenue George V. As far as he knew, the woman had vanished, leaving Dimitri to clean up her mess.

* * *

Florent's aunt Céline hosted her brother's wake at her mansion on the Bay of Biscay. The massive neoclassical house smelled of butter and sugar, which was fitting for the Cookie Tsarina of Brittany. The only bright side to Pierre's death was that it had left Florent a millionaire. Not anywhere near the immense wealth of his aunt, but enough to get a comfortable start to life, which was good, since Florent was headed to college in Geneva in the fall.

He picked up a fresh butter cookie and walked into the garden, staring out at the lapis-colored waves as the sun began its path to sleep. His aunt tiptoed behind him and rested her hand on his back.

"*Mon chéri*," she said, "I am very sorry about your papa. I will miss him so."

Pierre sneered, "That's the way the cookie crumbles, right, Tata?"

"Do not let this experience turn you into a cynic, Florent." Her face hung in an odd way, with one eyelid drooping down. "Nobody likes a cynic." She fixed her face into its normal shape and trotted off.

Nobody likes a cynic, Florent repeated in his head. *Good thing I don't give a damn about being liked.*

He crushed the cookie with his hardening fist and tossed it into the ocean.

Though his grief howled through him like an angry wind, a singular thought drowned out all the others: *I must find Gia.*

6

July 30th

Moussa laid on the catamaran's net, suspended over the Atlantic Ocean, observing the rocking waves below him. The sun warmed his back, and he twisted his locs up on his head to invite the sunshine onto his neck.

The five months since he'd lost Oumar had stretched out like a fog, and he'd floated in that dark cloud alone, feeling totally disengaged from the world around him.

Queen Awa had considered sending him to a psychiatrist in Dakar for antidepressants. None of the ancient herbs she had treated him with had worked, and no matter how hard she tried, she could not snap him out of his depression.

"Queen Awa, what can I do for him, to help him?" Gia stood in the salon of the yacht, watching Moussa as he lay listless on the deck.

"I don't know, Gia. He's lost the love of his life. I don't think there's anything anyone can do."

Gia felt her stomach twist. Losing Cameron had been hard enough for her, but Oumar and Moussa had spent lifetimes together. She could not even imagine what that was like, not really. Rather than wrestle any further with her latent guilt over the death of Oumar, Gia turned her attention to her favorite subject: business. "What has happened with my casino in Macau?"

"As you suspected, Q was unable to transfer ownership of the land deed, so it remains in your name. However, we have not been able to locate the funds he took from the vaults."

Gia sighed and rubbed her temples. "When I saw the last accounting from Yiannis, we had eight hundred and twenty-two million Macanese Pataca...around eighty-seven million euros."

"Yes," the queen nodded. "That is correct."

"And it is all gone?"

"Every cent."

Gia closed her eyes and shook her head. "*Lo ucciderei di nuovo!*"

"I don't speak Italian."

"What I meant to say is that I would rip the heart out of that goddamn rotten psychopath if I were able. Slitting his throat was far too kind. I should have made him suffer more."

"That's Man for you. Mankind is nothing but a parasite on this planet," Queen Awa sighed.

Gia regarded the queen's tone and narrowed her eyes. "Is there more bad news?" she winced, preparing for the worst.

"We have not been able to wrestle control of the club in Argentina from Q's South American narco friend."

Gia collapsed onto the sofa, and Queen Awa followed shortly thereafter.

Gia looked at the queen squarely in her eyes. "The net loss in Argentina... it is what? Sixty thousand euros per month?"

"Roughly, a little more, maybe sixty-two thousand. Plus the cost of the real estate itself, which is—"

"Five million euros."

"More actually... six point two million."

Gia gritted her teeth and let out a breathy groan.

"Is there any good news at all?"

Queen Awa shook her head, "No, and in fact there is something else we need to discuss, because it will require the right strategy."

Gia braced herself for yet another financial blow.

"Gia, I received news from my friend João, the president of the mermaid colony in Brazil. He told me that Queen Zale has instructed her people to move against you."

That was news Gia had not expected and it made her spring upright.

"What does that mean?"

"Your cousin Yiannis and all your other family in Greece are coming after your empire."

7

August 2nd

Goldie Stern's office overlooked Times Square. Fifty stories below, a tall man in an Elmo costume groped the buttocks of a tourist taking a paid selfie with him. A nearly-nude cowboy and matching cowgirl strummed on guitars, singing patriotic songs like it was still the Fourth of July. Tourists stood in the middle of the street gawping at skyscrapers. In other words, it was your average Monday morning in central Manhattan.

Goldie scooted his wheelchair away from the window and angled it toward his desk. On the other side of the desk sat Harper.

"Your ratings are slipping, Harper." Goldie's voice was gruff, and he spoke through heavy, wet coughs. "I can't have that."

"I understand." And Harper did understand. She had gotten used to pulling in big numbers. The past year had been the most pivotal in her career, and the most tragic in her personal life.

"Your parents are leaving good material on the cutting room floor. I can see why. The murder of your brother must be very hard on them. But, Harper... that Mermaid story is gold. We have to exploit it for everything it's worth. Don't you agree?"

Do I agree? she wondered. She wasn't sure anymore. Maybe she was losing some of the fire in her belly, just like her parents.

"What are you proposing exactly, Goldie?"

"I don't want to tell you the ungodly sum that I spent acquiring the Mermaid Tape. My wife hasn't gotten over it yet. For heaven's sake, you'd think the woman has enough Birkin bags and Louboutin heels at this point. Do you know she wants to have *another* baby? My sixth child from five different mothers. I'm too old for that. I'm teetering into Alec Baldwin territory at this point. She keeps talking about college tuition for this phantom child. At this rate, I'll have to live to one hundred and fifty to pay for it all. But I digress... look, I *need* you to use your connection to Gia Acquaviva."

She inhaled sharply and tilted her head inquisitively. "In what way?"

"Don't be obtuse, Harper. You do understand that I can cut you at any time, right? There are many people who would be more than happy if I brought back Monica Yung. Your contract allows me to terminate you whenever I like. Without severance."

"Oh, I'm well aware. It's a risk I took in coming over to LION."

"I took a risk, too... in betting on you. And I don't like losing, get it? So, call up your sister-in-law, Gia, in Italy or wherever and pump her for information. Start covering the Nico murder again. Whatever it takes!"

"I have another idea." Harper leaned over Goldie's desk. His eyes caught a glimpse of her cleavage and he felt himself getting hard. He wheeled his chair back slightly and put his hand on the zipper of his pants, causing Harper to jump back in revulsion. "Goldie!" she screamed. "What the hell! That's not what I meant! Keep it in your pants! I'm talking about an exclusive interview!"

Goldie rolled back under his desk to cover his fading erection. At another point in his life, he would have been highly offended that she rebuffed him, but these days, after a string of sexual harassment lawsuits and all of that #MeToo nonsense, he didn't have the energy to be angry, only slightly annoyed.

"Hmmpf," he mumbled. "I like the word *exclusive.*" He sat in silence for a while, searching for ideas, but none came. "Listen, I don't care what you do, just get those goddamn numbers up. That will be all, Harper. Have yourself a lovely little week."

8

August 3rd

Queen Zale glanced around the table at her council. Having never left the colony, she knew very little of the world above the waves. Certainly, she'd read books and reviewed reports about humans and their activities on land, but she had no desire to interact with Man. Running her colony, overseeing the Pan-Atargatic Council for the last few hundred years, and convening with the Gracious Tides had been more than enough to keep her occupied. Therefore, she had a limited understanding of Gia's business dealings, as Yiannis described them.

"...And that is why I suggest we start with targeting Gia's club in Sydney," Yiannis concluded.

Queen Zale realized that, at some point in the last half hour when he had been speaking, she had tuned out and was now completely lost.

"Do you feel that is the best strategy, Your Majesty?" he asked her, clearly wanting her blessing for his plans.

She cleared her throat and squared her shoulders. "If you feel this is the way forward, I shall give you all the support you need," she replied, masking her confusion with a veneer of equanimity.

"Perfect, then I shall arrange for Prince Bryce and Prince Kyle to come to us as soon as possible."

"The Princes of California?" Queen Zale asked—not so much as to find out anything specific, but rather to see if she could jog her memory and retrieve even the slightest detail of the plan Yiannis had laid out. Unfortunately, her mind was blank. "Very well," she continued. "Perhaps we can revisit our conversations on oceanic violence while the Princes are here."

"Excellent idea, Ma'am. Leave it with me." Yiannis bowed and left the queen's chambers along with the other members of her council.

Once she was alone, she opened the door to her private chapel, knelt, and began to pray. "O Gracious Tides bless the Nations of Atargatis, we are few."

The carved chamber filled with water, enveloping her in a cold embrace. The tide spoke to Queen Zale, "Child of the sea, our pearl of creation, you are blessed and loved."

"I come to You, this day, for Your aid. The child of the sea and spawn of clay, Gia Acquaviva... I know not how to proceed with her. I beg of You to show me the way forward. She chose her punishment... she chose excommunication... and in doing so, she chose the clay. Help me understand Your will, so that I may guide my people. I fear dark days ahead for the world of Mermaid."

9

August 3rd

Gia was sleeping when the yacht began to pitch. The wind whipped the sails of the catamaran out of their ropes, and the canvases unfurled against the night sky. The captain shouted into the ship's radio, "All hands on deck!" He instructed the crew to act quickly and tie everything down.

The skipper woke Gia. "Miss Acquaviva, we are experiencing some rough weather. We'd like you to put on a life jacket as a precaution."

"A life jacket?" She shook her head several times to rouse herself from her dreams. "I do not require a life jacket. I am a mermaid, remember?"

The boat lurched violently to the left, and the skipper lost his balance, slamming against the wall of Gia's suite. His head hit the smooth wood, and he was knocked unconscious, falling limply to the floor. Gia froze. The position of his body on the carpet made her recall how her mother had died so many years before, oozing blood onto the deck of her father's small yacht. Gia stood in place, staring at him, waiting for blood to leak from his head, just like it had from her mamma's. But there was none.

Up on the deck, the crew screamed at one another, frantically tying things down and trying to shift weight here and there, so that the boat would not capsize. With every passing second, the ocean churned more forcefully. Gia climbed out of the belly of the ship to see that, despite the surging waves, there was no rain, which seemed odd. The storm had struck seemingly from nowhere. The boat had been silent and still, but—within mere minutes—the sea had become a monster. Gia registered terror on the faces of the crew members. Her security team sheltered in place in their accommodations below deck.

"Incoming wave!" someone yelled.

Water splashed onto the boat in a straight sheet. Gia ran back downstairs and gathered her personal items, including money and her burner phone, and threw them into a waterproof bag, which she placed in a backpack. She then strapped the backpack over her shoulders, securing it around her waist

Gia had acted not a moment too soon, because another giant wave sliced through the center of the boat like a machete, splitting it open. The yacht may as well have been a piñata. The contents of the boat, along with all the people on it, went spilling into the water like cheap candy.

The current held onto Gia and dragged her down into the deep sea. Twisting round and round, it felt like she was in the grip of a witch's bony hand, and the freezing Atlantic water squeezed her at the waist.

The strong hand of the current pulled her through a crevice in the rocks, and her backpack got caught in the narrow passageway. She was able to use the opposite force to begin breaking free from the water spiral. Beating her tail furiously, she finally pushed through the rocks and wrapped her body around the craggy wall, grasping at slippery plants. After much effort, she was able to wriggle her way onto the seafloor and take cover in a kelp forest, tying herself down at the arm with a long stalk of seaweed.

Never in her life had she experienced such a strange assault from the ocean. She laid in the thrashing seaweed for a long time, recharging and watching the motion around her slow. When life underwater once again swayed with lazy ease, she swam away.

Gia's abrupt descent had left her disoriented. It was dark under the surface, and even though she could see from the glowing of her eyes, her night vision wasn't much help. She swam in what she felt might be the direction of the coast. It must have been hours later when sunlight finally broke, and she surfaced.

In this distance she could see waves breaking against a concrete structure and she continued forward. The waves here were three stories high and brave surfers rode them. However, when she spotted the fire-engine-red lighthouse on the shore, Gia immediately knew that she had landed in Nazare, Portugal. Home of record-breaking surf.

She climbed out of the ocean via a tall, metal ladder that dropped her at the top of a cliff. But no one saw her. Anyone standing on the platform near the lighthouse had their eyes trained on the surfers.

Once she caught her breath, she unstrapped the battered backpack, unsealed the waterproof bag inside and pulled out the burner phone. It was bone dry and unscathed.

She dialed *La Nonna* to arrange for swift transportation to a safe location.

10

August 10th

Serena bobbed up and down in the kitchen's large apron sink. Royce and Bronwyn stood over the merbaby, transfixed. The past two weeks had been surreal and rather horrifying for the couple. The baby's tail was stubborn in its mission to *exist*, and they had not seen her skinny little legs for so long.

The pediatrician had been a bust. He was stumped, and essentially threw his hands up when they'd sought his advice. "She's not human. I can't help you," he'd told them.

They saw another doctor, and another. No one helped them. In desperation, they turned to a marine biologist, an expert on salmon no less. He had at least some useful information for them and suggested that they keep Serena in saline water. The marine biologist also gave them some nutritional supplements that he often fed to baby salmon. No doubt, Serena had perked up since that consultation.

Thus far, the Langleys had managed to grease palms thoroughly enough as to stay under the radar, and the situation they were facing with their "grandfish" had not yet been detected by the press—a reprieve they knew couldn't last forever. As far as the global media was concerned, Gia was either still pregnant or was on the lam with her tiny mermaid. It was Bronwyn's goal to maintain that fiction for as long as possible.

* * *

HARPER HAD NOT SPOKEN to her parents in weeks. Ever since the meeting in Goldie's office, Harper had been texting her mother every day to check in, hoping for an opening, a thawing in her mother's ice. Thus far, her parents had been reluctant to allow Harper access, and on some level she understood. She knew they didn't want to be "part of the news"... unless they could control the narrative, that is. And Harper, being the face of a competitive news channel now simply wasn't a safe bet to keep within the inner circle.

Therefore, it came as a real surprise to Harper when her mother rang her up on a random Tuesday morning for lunch at the manor.

"It's time for you to meet your niece," Bronwyn had said on the phone. "This is what Cam-Cam would want, Harper."

As Harper left her apartment on the Upper West Side and sped up the West Side Highway toward her parents' house, she felt uneasy about the family get-together.

Am I seriously supposed to pretend that this is normal? A mermaid baby? This whole thing feels like the Addams Family or some kind of made-up shit like Bat Baby.

She needed a distraction.

Harper spoke aloud to the virtual assistant on her phone, "Hey, Lila, start Cam's playlist." The car stereo pumped out her brother's favorite pop songs. He'd created the playlist the last time they took a long car trip together a few years before. She mouthed the words to a Selena Gomez song and found herself both incredibly sad and very amused by her brother's pedestrian taste in music.

She took a breath and held it in until her chest ached. She did this a few times, and it left her light-headed. Part of her wished she'd pass out and crash her car into the median. At least she'd be finished with all the stress in her life and get to be with Cam again.

"This is fucking unfair, Cam!" she screamed. "How could you leave me alone with Mom and Dad? That was not the deal we made!"

Had Cameron been given the choice, he would have opted for a long life with loud music, laughter, and lots of good food. Cam had a way of bringing out the best in Harper, and she knew, deep in her soul, that he had been the better person. *He* was the one who really deserved to be alive. Harper zoned out, lost in memories of her big brother.

* * *

BRONWYN HAD NEVER BEEN a fan of eating in the kitchen. To her, it felt like something poor people do, because they don't have enough furniture. She much preferred a more formal setting, either the breakfast table, or the dining room in the evenings. However, since baby Serena seemed happiest in the kitchen sink, Bronwyn had the chef prepare tea and finger sandwiches, served at the large marble island. Bronwyn took a seat on a barstool and watched the baby as she floated in the water.

"Mom?" Harper shouted, as she cracked open the front door.

"We're in the kitchen, Harpie."

Harper took her time walking in. She knew that this was one of those rare moments in life that would leave a notch on the timeline: before and after Mermaid Langley. She pushed the kitchen's swinging door and took a step into an uncertain future.

Naturally, Serena's golden tail was the first thing Harper saw. It was ridged and delicate, wispy at the ends, like a dandelion blowing in the wind. The human half of the child looked remarkably like Harper herself, light blonde hair and big blue eyes. Harper had expected to feel disgust, but there wasn't an ounce of derision when she looked at this tiny being. On the contrary, Harper felt that she could stand in place forever, staring at her niece. The child was a thing of beauty and grace.

"Do you want to hold her?" Bronwyn asked. "I can take her out of the water."

"No, no... don't bother her. She looks so relaxed."

"She loves the sink."

"What do you do with her at night?"

Bronwyn hid her face in her hands. "I can't even say it."

Harper turned her eyes toward her mother. "Mom, what? Say it."

"Do you remember that pedicure tub your father got me for Christmas a few years ago?"

"Of course," Harper laughed. "You were mad at him for weeks for buying that. He has no talent for gift giving."

"Well, I found a use for it," Bronwyn admitted, her voice thick. "I fill it up with saline water and put it next to my side of the bed, and that's where the baby sleeps. I'm still afraid she's going to drown."

Harper snorted, picturing the scene. "I don't think that's possible, Mom."

"Well, how would I know?" Bronwyn snapped. "The truth is I am absolutely exhausted."

"Don't you have a night nurse?"

"I don't feel comfortable leaving her alone with anyone right now. What if someone took her?"

Harper sat down next to her mother. "You look terrible. Why don't you lie down while I watch her?"

Bronwyn's eyes glistened. "Would you, darling? Would you, please? There is nothing I would love more than a hot bath and an hour to myself."

"Of course."

"Oh, Harper!" Bronwyn wrapped her arms around her daughter. "I'm so glad you're here. I've missed you. I really have, my darling."

Harper wasn't used to this level of affection from her mother, and she resisted the urge to return the hug. "Mmm," Harper hummed, peeling herself away, "you got it!"

Bronwyn tickled Serena's cheek and then slipped out the door.

Harper rose from her chair and looked around, to make sure she was really alone with Serena.

"Kiddo," she said, "it's just you and me."

Harper slipped her hand into her purse and snuck her phone out, flicking the camera to video mode. "Auntie Harper loves you. Now, sweetie, smile for the camera."

11

May 1995

Florent huddled in the alleyway, near the back entrance to La Perle Noire. Music from inside the cabaret made its way outside when the door opened. Florent's eyes scanned every face that he saw, hoping to find Gia's.

He loitered in the shadows, long enough for the music to stop, the tables to be cleaned, and the dancers to wash off their makeup.

When he finally spotted Dimitri, he felt overcome with rage. Dimitri rounded the corner, and Florent grabbed him by the collar and slammed him against the wall.

"Where is she?" Florent cried.

Dimitri, startled, pushed Florent off of him and shoved him backward. "What the fuck is wrong with you, Florent? You scared me half to death."

"Where is Gia? You *must* have seen her."

Rolling his eyes ever so briefly at the theatrics, Dimitri reached for Florent's hand and asked, "Why don't you come back to the apartment with me?"

"I can't go back there!"

"I am so sorry about your father. Come here." Dimitri pulled Florent in for a hug, and the young man collapsed into the arms of his former lover.

* * *

Dimitri poured Florent a glass of red wine. They drank together, solemnly, on the sofa. Florent took stock of everything in the room. The table where he'd done lines of coke and fucked Gia. The stain on the wall where his father had smashed his glass of bourbon.

Florent's shame twisted inside of him, its blade slicing through everything. His pain was unbearable.

Dimitri studied Florent's face—he really was so handsome. And shattered. The heaviness of grief only made Florent appear more attractive, because the grief overshadowed his most unattractive quality—his arrogance.

Dimitri reached out and stroked Florent's cheek.

"Don't fucking touch me!" Florent snapped, slapping Dimitri's hand away.

Dimitri eased back, retreating to the corner of the couch.

"I have not heard a single word from Gia," Dimitri finally said, in a whisper. "She disappears like this sometimes, you see." Dimitri sighed and gulped his wine.

Florent hung his head.

"What do you want from her anyway, Florent?"

"I just need to speak with her, that's all."

Dimitri considered the answer and then pressed, "To say what?"

"Not to say anything! To ask her *why*. Why did she fuck my father over like that?"

"Florent, darling, we *all* did that to him. Believe me, it is messing with my head, also, but—"

"Stop it. It was a mistake coming here." Florent chugged what was left of his wine and slammed his glass on the table. He averted his eyes from the patio door, from the scene of the accident. He sprang out of the apartment, rushed down the stairs, and burst out onto Avenue George V. His brain flashed with images of his father's mangled body on the concrete, and he doubled over, screaming with pain. But not a sound escaped. He beat his chest over and over until tears filled his eyes and spilled out onto his cheeks.

I did this. I killed my father. No, we did. Me, Dimitri, and Gia. Why has she disappeared? Why did she leave me alone to deal with this? Didn't she have any feelings for me? Or, is this what she wanted all along... to fuck my father and kill him? Was I just part of some sick plan? Gia, where are you?

12

August 12th

Gia threw a pile of bread into the chicken coop and walked back into the villa.

Portuguese bread is the worst.

She longed for a decent ciabatta or a crusty baguette. What was the point of hiding out at an olive farm in a podunk village without delicious carbs to dip into aged olive oil? Not to mention, she hated Portuguese cuisine in general. Canned sardines? Disgusting. She'd survived the past few weeks on steamed vegetables and fresh fruit.

Her burner phone buzzed, bouncing on the dining room table. She answered it, feeling impatient and on edge.

"I hope you have an update for me on my custody case," Gia barked, her way of greeting her lawyer.

"*Bene, allora,*" *La Nonna* said nervously, "turn on the television."

"*Vecchia*, you know I do not like puzzle games. Tell me what is happening."

"Your... sister-in-law... she has released footage of Serena. It debuted on her evening program last night, and now it is on every channel."

Gia flipped on the flat screen, and indeed, on every channel that covered news, the talking heads were blabbering about "The Little Mermaid," as they had so inelegantly dubbed her. Camera crews had set up outside Langley Manor, but everyone knew Harper was the only reporter with the inside scoop, so they had no choice but to roll her footage over and over. She'd even released a statement *begging* the media to grant her parents some privacy. Oh, the irony of it all.

Gia's heart thumped, and her eyes watered. Seeing her baby floating in a kitchen sink like a dirty sponge upset her deeply.

"What are they *doing* to my baby?" she howled, mostly to herself.

"I have filed for an emergency custody hearing with the court," *La Nonna* replied, "but without you present, I think our chances of advancing the case are not good."

"In other words, these monsters are able to keep my child from me? If the authorities in Venice have dismissed the murder charges against me, why am I not able to leave? I want to go to New York as soon as possible."

"I have a plan. There is a judge who is... how should I describe him? He is *sympathetic* to your circumstances. He is someone I have known for a very long time. I have been working with some individuals I know to catapult him into the judiciary, and in a few weeks, he will be moved into a position that will be highly advantageous for us. He has agreed to make a public statement that should clear things up for you."

"This is highly unusual. I thought judges do not make such declarations."

"He is a highly *unusual* man... with highly *unusual* tastes, you see. He is aware that I know of his peculiarities, and he is willing to do quite a lot for me in order to protect his reputation. Once he issues this statement, it will be very difficult for any prosecutor in Italy to bring a case against you regarding Nico."

"I see. And when do you expect this to happen?"

"At the latest... a month or so from now. Then you shall be free to again walk the streets anywhere with your two sexy legs, *angioletta*."

"Then what?"

"*Signorina* Acquaviva, then we travel to New York and go *tête-à-tête* with the grandparents."

13

August 25th

The line to get into Oasis snaked down the block. Incessant reporting on The Little Mermaid story had revived interest in all of Gia's establishments. This was particularly true of the Sydney-based Oasis club—and *The Late Show with Stephen Colbert* had placed a manned crew outside its front door during evening hours. Colbert was doing a running bit called "Mermaids Down Under," where local drag queens, dressed as mermaids, interviewed drunk people.

On that particular evening, one of the drag superstars had come dressed as Queen Awa. No one knew she was a queen, of course, they simply knew her as the "Black mermaid who helped save Gia from the tank in Sicily."

However, the *real* Queen Awa was also present on site, and she was not amused. She observed the commotion outside via the security cameras, while remaining ensconced in the club's cushy, soundproof office. She rested her forehead in her palms and let her mind wander.

Two hundred years in power, and what I am now known for is plucking that nuisance of a mermaid out of an insane man's vanity aquarium? This is undoubtedly a low point.

Oh, but, indeed, the bottom had an even steeper drop. And Queen Awa had no idea how low things would actually go. She peeked through her hands to look at the security screens and saw police officers push past the bouncers. One of her Senegalese subjects, who was moonlighting as a cocktail waiter, sprinted to the office and banged on the door.

"Open the door, please, Your Majesty!"

Queen Awa flicked open the lock and let the merperson in.

"We are being raided!"

"Raided?!" the queen replied, confused.

"The police are arresting underage people."

"But aren't the bouncers checking identification?"

"Yes, of course. But apparently there are more than fifty high school students in here."

Queen Awa burst in the main hall to see young people being rounded up and escorted out into paddy wagons. And then, glancing up to the second floor balcony, she saw two smug faces that she knew all too well.

Prince Kyle and Prince Bryce of California each raised a martini glass in salute to Awa.

She flashed a fake smile and nodded at them.

So, those nasty little catfish are behind this scheme. How dare the Greeks use these matching nitwits to come after me. I wonder if their mother knows about this? Is she cooperating with Queen Zale? I will get to the bottom of this. Either way, Queen Karen is going to get an earful from me. Zale has severely underestimated me as an enemy. She has made a grave miscalculation. In time she will understand how very wrong she is.

14

September 13th

Outside the Langleys' house, camera crews from every news station imaginable were staked out, hoping for a glimpse of Serena, The Little Mermaid. However, Royce and Bronwyn hadn't left the walls of their fortress in days—not since Harper released the footage of baby Serena in the kitchen sink.

In addition to the reporters, a new set of agitators had begun appearing on the scene: activists from a group called ADET, Animals Deserve Equal Treatment. The group was known for its anarchist approach to animal welfare. ADET members frequently did things like break into cattle farms to capture disturbing video and then release the herds. Much to the chagrin of the neighbors, ADET had erected tents alongside the road in the tony Hudson Valley village near the Langleys' estate. Every time the police asked them to move, more activists showed up, and the campsite simply migrated and expanded outward.

Inside the manor, just after three o'clock in the morning, Serena howled and woke Bronwyn from a fitful sleep. She leapt out of bed and rushed over to Serena's makeshift aqua-bassinet to check on the baby, who flopped around restlessly.

Bronwyn tried plugging the pedicure tub into the wall so that the water would bubble up from the jets. She'd found that Serena enjoyed the bubbles, and this often soothed her and stopped her from crying, but not tonight.

Many weeks ago Royce had taken to sleeping in the guest room. He did not enjoy having his granddaughter disrupt his slumber. So, Bronwyn need not worry about waking a grumpy husband when she switched on her bedside lamp.

But when she turned back around to face the baby, she gasped.

Serena's golden tail was lackluster, and her scales appeared to be flaking off. If the baby had been a goldfish, she might have been doomed to a toilet flush. Bronwyn touched Serena's forehead, and it was burning up. The baby wouldn't stop screaming.

Bronwyn reached for her cell phone and dialed the marine biologist. As a joke, Royce had saved the man's number in his wife's phone under the moniker of "Dr. Salmon."

The line trilled, but after a moment she heard an automated message saying that the voicemail had not been set up. She tried again and again, but he didn't answer. It was the middle of the night, and he likely had his phone set to Do Not Disturb, because he didn't respond to her texts either.

Bronwyn picked up the crying baby and rocked her, but the wails were incessant. Serena even managed to rouse Royce, despite the fact that he was halfway across the house with earplugs in.

He stomped into the room and began shouting. "What in the hell is wrong with the baby? She hasn't stopped crying for a half hour!"

"Royce, she's really sick. She's running a fever, and look at her tail! It's practically grey!"

He shot a quick sideways glance at the merbaby. "Well, what does Dr. Salmon say?"

"He's not answering my calls!"

"Shit! So what are you going to do?"

"Me?! What am *I* going to do? You're her grandfather for God's sake. Can't you help her?"

"How am I supposed to help?"

"My God, Royce! I will not lose this baby! Do you hear me?! I will not! Think of something! Otherwise I'm going to have to drive her to the hospital... through that thick wall of reporters outside. And neither of us wants to be captured on camera right now."

He shuffled around in circles, his head struggling to formulate a plan, which was a very difficult thing to do with a newborn screaming at the top of her lungs next to him. He had once done a story on dolphin trainers in New Jersey. Perhaps there was something there? After several minutes he realized that he was engaging in a fruitless exercise in futility. He'd already tapped every ocean-related contact worth their salt. There wasn't a soul left in his rolodex who could help them.

Except for one.

"Darling," he gritted his teeth, preparing for what came next, "you're not going to like this..."

Bronwyn glared at him, her rage louder than the shrieking baby she held.

"I think," he winced, "we have to call *La Nonna*."

But Bronwyn was already shaking her head. "I'm not giving this baby to Gia, Royce! I won't do it!"

"Jesus Christ, woman, I'm not saying you have to!"

Bronwyn's eyes filled with tears, and she sat on the edge of the bed.

He steadied himself on the mahogany bedpost. "Look, maybe... and this a real *maybe*, darling... maybe she will help us."

Bronwyn looked down at Serena's miserable little face and felt overcome with helplessness. "Fine. Call her."

He dialed the Italian cell phone number, and within a minute, he had *La Nonna* on the line.

"*Buon giorno*, *Signor* Langley!" she said, as she answered her phone. "It is quite late in New York is it not?"

"Let's cut to the chase, *La Nonna*. The baby is sick, and we need your help."

"I see," she replied, smiling. "I am certain that we can help each other, *Signor* Langley."

La Nonna had already laid the groundwork for this moment, because she, very cleverly, had anticipated that the Langleys would become overwhelmed while taking care of Serena. Now they were exactly where she wanted them. All *La Nonna* had to do was snap her fingers and Gia would be in the perfect offensive position, ready to fight.

15

September 15th

Flying over the Atlantic, Gia's brain buzzed with a thousand thoughts. Top of mind, of course, was Serena.

My baby must be very sick if the Langleys reached out to La Nonna for help. I would be the last resort.

She worried about her business, too. She was hemorrhaging cash at the moment. The Greek-Californian alliance had succeeded in getting her Australian liquor license temporarily suspended. The casino in Macau was still pretty much non-functional. Queen Awa was doing her best to plug the holes, but she simply did not have vast experience running this type of multinational organization, unlike Gia and Yiannis.

And speaking of her cousin, Yiannis was the worst person for her to face off against as she tried to regain control, because he knew every weakness in the business.

And then there was Florent.

She couldn't deny the shock she had felt seeing him again after so long... but there was something else, too.

A sinister tingling.

For Gia, seeing that scar slashed across his throat had given her intense erotic pleasure. She sifted in her seat thinking about how exhilarating it had been to rip into his flesh all those years ago.

Glancing around the lounge of her jet, she noticed that the security staff seemed relaxed and distracted. She reached over and pulled a cashmere Hermès blanket over her lap and angled her body toward the window.

Sometimes when she masturbated, she flicked through her "greatest hits"—her favorite kills—and today was no exception. Her hand slipped past the elastic waistband of her silk harem pants, landing on top of her lace panties. She thought first of Nico. He was so good, his murder had been perfectly executed. He'd melted into her dominance in exactly the way he always had, in precisely the way she wanted. She pictured his face, eyes closed, and neck extended backward, tense with wanting her. Then her mind flashed to Josh, her first kill, and the sweet rush of endorphins that bubbled up when slicing through his muscles.

The pads of her fingers massaged her clit, and she made the tiniest of motions with her hips. She remembered another lover, one that she'd tied up on a boat in the basement of an abandoned palazzo in Venice. She had cut him only enough to stop him from talking, but he had remained very much alive—at least for a little while. She had watched him die slowly, blood dripping down his naked chest, spilling onto his manhood between his legs.

Gia bit her lip and felt her pulse rise as she came, finally relaxing into her seat. Then, she fell into a peaceful sleep.

* * *

La Nonna met Gia on the tarmac at Teterboro. From New Jersey, they hopped in a chopper that would transport them to the heliport on the other side of the Hudson River, where a motorcade worthy of a European prime minister escorted them to a celebrity-favored hotel on 77th between 5th and Madison. After driving into the garage below the building, Gia and her team were whisked away to the top floor without ever being spotted.

At a whopping seventy-five thousand dollars a night, the establishment's Grand Penthouse definitely lived up to its name. Gia excused the hotel's butler and poured herself four fingers of bourbon on the rocks before collapsing onto a sofa under the living room's cathedral ceiling.

"*Bene, allora,*" *La Nonna* began, "shall we speak about business now or after you finish your tiny little beverage?"

Gia shot her a nasty look. "Why is it that you are always making jokes? Is your humor supposed to relax people? Do you think it makes you more charming?"

"*Signorina* Acquaviva," *La Nonna* let out an incredulous chuckle, "is it not a better way to behave than offending everyone with a highly unpleasant and sour attitude?"

"Get on with it, then," Gia replied, tipping the glass into her mouth and letting the slightly sweet burn of the booze travel down. "I would like to see my daughter as soon as possible, and I notice that you have your Gucci briefcase on your lap, so I imagine it contains a plan of some sort."

"My, how observant we are this evening." *La Nonna* popped the lock on the briefcase and pulled out some papers, reading through them. "You, *angioletta*, are famous—world famous—in fact. Fame brings both misfortune and opportunity. I would like to focus on the latter."

Fame? Gia thought. *It is a curse.*

The fact of the matter was that Gia's bad mood was the result of the whole mess of what it meant simply *to be* who she was now. She longed for the past, when she could walk without the flash of paparazzi cameras or the filthy ogling of anonymous cell phones.

What is it Americans love to say so much? Ah, yes... 'It is what it is.' As much joy as his murder brought me, killing Nico was not worth losing my freedom.

La Nonna snapped her finger at Gia. "*Scusami!* We have work to do. I need your full attention."

Gia was too tired to sass the old woman, so she just nodded like a robot.

"Tomorrow morning I have arranged a meeting with the top PR agent in New York. Talia Levi is her name. She will handle our media strategy."

"Media strategy?" Gia groaned.

"Absolutely!" *La Nonna* threw up her hands. "*Madonna!* It is as if you know nothing, understand nothing! America *loves* celebrities. And there is only one thing that America loves more than celebrities... a thing they call 'an apology tour'."

16

September 16th

"Are you both insane?" Gia screamed. "An animal hospital?! You want to take my daughter to an *animal* hospital?"

Opposite Gia, across the concrete dining table in the hotel's Grand Penthouse, sat *La Nonna* and the black-bobbed, *très* petite Talia Levi.

"*Angioletta*," *La Nonna* pleaded, "listen to the woman. Her plan is perfect."

"Gia, honey," Talia said, adjusting her enormous, zebra-print glasses, "I'm in the storytelling business. Mkay? You're like... literally... a mythical creature. Basically a goddess, all right? So, is it horrific to send your daughter to Manhattan Animal Emergency Hospital? Yeah. Yeah, it is. She's, like... gonna be next to some ten-year-old chihuahua getting a hysterectomy. And that's great! Because why? Because of Klik Klak."

Gia lasered her eyes toward *La Nonna* and began cursing loudly at her in Italian before returning her gaze to Talia. "What the *hell* is Klik Klak?"

Talia's eyes bugged. "Are you serious?"

"I am losing my patience," Gia said, tapping her foot against the leg of her chair. "Make this make sense to me, or I will have you both escorted out. I will then drive myself to the Langleys' house, remove Serena, and dive immediately into the Hudson."

"Fuckin' A! Well, we can't have that. Let me start from the top. Mkay?" Talia pushed up the puffy pink sleeves of her crêpe de chine silk blouse. "What we want is to create a frenzy... this country is crazy divided at the mo', and we want to take advantage of that. So, what we're gonna do is to use—" Talia leaned over for dramatic effect and whispered the next words, "*social media* to make you look like a Disney Princess come to life. Do you follow me?"

Gia cocked her head, "A Disney Princess?"

Talia ignored Gia and continued her strategizing. "Great. So. Klik Klak is, like, the tippy top of the most popular social media platforms at the mo'. I've already done extensive social listening, and what I've discovered is that a growing number of folks, especially left-wing animal rights activists, feel that the Langleys are not, like, the right fit to raise a merbaby."

"Which is obvious," Gia muttered to herself.

"I heard that," Talia snapped. "Look, tbh, it's *not* that obvious to *a whole lot* of people. I don't know if you've been paying attention to what's happening in this country, but there's, like, a whole conversation about race going on. For example, there are a ton of people who don't think that Black children should be adopted by White families who don't have close relationships with Black people. There's a parallel there with the mermaid thing. That's what I call a 'tap-in moment'. Because, like, the Langleys... they're literally everything that's wrong with this country. They're trying to White-savior this merbaby, and that's fucked up, and that's the story we're gonna get out there."

Gia looked past Talia to *La Nonna*, "I do not understand anything she is talking about."

La Nonna shrugged. "Her argument is quite solid according to the case law. But as I told you, our best chance is to win custody in the court of public opinion. These days, more than ever before, cases are won and lost in the media."

"Totes," Talia clucked. "So, I've got a stylist coming in to fit you with a bunch of new *lewks*. All cream everything. And sparkles, so many sparkles. She'll be here in thirty minutes. Then we're gonna go to Manhattan Animal Emergency Hospital to meet the Langleys. I have this huge Klik Klaker coming to the hospital to do a livestream. It would be super great if you could cry while they're examining Serena. Also, question re: your tail... can you, like, summon it whenever?"

"Yes," Gia replied, flatly.

"Mkay, fab. Super useful. I'm envisioning a *'moment'* for that. Cool, then also I've set you up for a date tonight with a really hot girl."

Gia's face twisted up in confusion.

"Honey, fix your face. We gotta win over the queers. Nobody fights for their own like the queers. For serious. Also, you have that whole 'man-killer' vibe going, and it's not a good look. Like, it's actually a really *bad* look. Girlboss is over. We hate that energy. Mkay? Like, we need to fully 'Princess Diana' you. This woman I'm setting you up with tonight is a big up-and-coming movie star, and she's gonna be in a new action film next summer and needs to raise her profile. She's really cool. You're gonna love her... I mean, you don't have to, like, *actually love* her. You know what I mean. Definitely don't kill her though. LOL. Anyways, let's get you started with the glam team right now before the stylist arrives."

* * *

GIA OBSERVED the chaotic scene outside Manhattan Animal Emergency Hospital from an Escalade across the street. The media mosh pit somewhat resembled a zombie horde. Talia and *La Nonna* had arranged for the Langleys to arrive first. Genius, really, to chum the sharks like that.

The hospital had cordoned off the walkway to the front entrance, and NYPD officers maintained strong boundaries. Bronwyn wheeled a creepy English pram down the pathway. She'd covered the bassinet with a blanket to obscure Serena from the prying eyes of the press. The Langelys weren't dumb-dumbs, though. They'd been at the game long enough to know how to play offense. Royce walked behind Bronwyn accompanied by Ashley Mason, Harper's replacement, and a camera guy.

When Talia spotted the OTN crew with Royce, she snickered. "Amazing! They did *exactly* what I knew they would. It's not going to play well with like ninety-nine percent of the Internet that they're rolling up to the hospital with Ashley 'Mason-Dixon Line'."

She gave Gia the up-and-down, inspecting everything. Gia had been outfitted in a cream-colored wrap dress with romantic sleeves. The velvet piping on the dress had a bit of an iridescent sheen, which the stylist had matched to shiny, pearl encrusted strappy heels. Gia's long, dark hair had been set into loose Botticelli waves. The overall effect was absolutely angelic.

And the pièce de résistance? Layers of mascara that were in no way waterproof.

"Mkay!" Talia clapped. "It's showtime. Get your gameface on, Gia. Give me Meryl Streep in *Sophie's Choice*. Give me Susan Sarandon in *Stepmom*. OMG, no. I've got it. This is it... give me Sally Field in *Not Without My Daughter*. I want sadness, but also outrage. Mkay! Let's go."

Talia cracked open the car door, and Gia stepped out into the palm of America.

If Gia looked bewildered in the press photos from that day, it's because she truly was. She belonged in the shadows, not the spotlight. Little did she know that to the camera, her reticence looked like innocence.

Gia was accompanied by a security detail, who were celebrity-trained and schooled in the art of how not to block photo ops. Talia and *La Nonna* headed up the rear.

Once inside the lobby of the veterinary hospital, Team Gia came face-to-face with Team Langley. Ashley Mason was live on camera, broadcasting to conservative America.

Ashley accosted Gia with her microphone. "Gia, yesterday an Italian judge gave a press conference announcing that you had been cleared in the murder of Nico. How were you able to escape prosecution in Italy? Did you pay him off? How can you possibly take this poor child away from her loving grandparents and drop her into your depraved world of gambling, booze, and *murder*?"

Little did the Langleys know how much this stunt would backfire. In the corner, holding a cell phone tuned to Klik Klak Live, was Washi-Washi, the app's third-most-popular content creator.

Washi-Washi shouted at Ashley, "Hey, Ashley Mason-Dixon Line! Over here! Why haven't you addressed the rumors that your father is the Grand Master of your hometown chapter of the KKK?" Washi-Washi then sprayed her with a glitter gun and disappeared down the hall.

Royce panicked and signaled to Ashley to cut the feed.

Ashley spoke calmly to her viewers through the camera lens while shaking glitter out of her hair, "I will be filing both assault and defamation charges against that Internet punk. But for now, I will toss it back to the main studio. I'll be back to update you after a short break. And remember, folks, OTN is your only source for the simple truth in this complicated world."

La Nonna ushered Gia into a private room. Waiting inside, hidden from view, was Gia's OBGYN from the Greek mermaid colony, Dr. Kupolou. Gia felt intensely relieved to see the doctor's familiar face.

"We have to stop meeting like this," the doctor teased. "They're always such a circus around you. I don't know how you handle it."

Gia grabbed the doctor's hand and found that her own was trembling. "Doctor, have you seen my baby yet?"

"No, the arrangement is that the grandmother will bring her in here, and that it's only the three of us together when I examine Baby Serena." The doctor paused and considered Gia, taking in her appearance. "How are you feeling? Are you having any postpartum symptoms, any depression?"

"I do not think so. Only anxiety, a lot of anxiety. I want to be with my child."

"I can imagine, Gia," the doctor replied, her voice rich with kindness.

The door squeaked open, and the doctor took a step to the side in case there was a stray camera somewhere. In strode Bronwyn, holding onto Serena, who was wrapped in a blanket.

When Gia saw how pallid and sullen Bronwyn looked, her stomach dropped. Gia was desperate to hold her child, to get a glimpse of her. Bronwyn approached Dr. Kupolou with extreme caution.

"May I hold her?" the doctor asked, softly.

Bronwyn extended her arms, and Dr. Kupolou took hold of Serena. She laid the baby down on the stainless steel examination table and unwrapped the blankets. Serena's eyes were closed, and she moved very little. Her skin had a blue undertone, and her tail had faded from golden to light brown.

Gia felt her chest swell, as if a strong wave had knocked the wind out of her. "*Mia dolce bambina!*" she cried, rushing to touch Serena's curly-haired head.

Bronwyn winced and turned her head to keep from crying.

The doctor took Serena's vitals while asking Bronwyn questions about the daily feeding and care of the little mermaid.

"How much is she sleeping?"

"A normal amount," Bronwyn replied. "I think."

"And how often is she out in the air like this?"

"Almost never, really. I... I thought with the tail and everything, that she should be in the water as much as possible."

"Mmm, I see."

"Is that bad?" Bronwyn asked, breathless. "Should I keep her out of the water?"

"No, I think you've done the right thing there."

"And what are you feeding Serena?"

"We have a wet nurse."

The doctor's eyes flashed with panic. "Human breastmilk?"

"Yes."

"Anything else?"

"We also give her some supplements we got from a marine biologist."

"Supplements?"

"It's something he gives the baby salmon he works with."

"Fish food," the doctor noted that detail in a chart, a frown present on her face. "You're feeding Serena *fish food*?"

"I hadn't thought of it like that, but... yes, I suppose so. She seems to like it. Sometimes we mix it into the milk."

"It's really good that you brought Serena here, Mrs. Langley, because the diet you're giving her is making her sick. She's not getting the nutrients she needs, and it appears that she's having an allergic reaction, more than likely to the spirulina in the fish food. It's a freshwater algae that is highly toxic to mermaids. Honestly, it could have killed her if you'd waited even a few days more."

Bronwyn began shaking, and she clenched her jaw shut, but it didn't stop the tears from welling up in her eyes. "I didn't know."

"Of course you did not know!" Gia exploded. "How dare you take my child from me! You have no idea how to care for her. You nearly killed my baby." Gia's gills cut against the muscles inside her arms. She ached to slice into Bronwyn, but kept her cool.

Dr. Kupolou waved her hands in between the two women. "I know this is very upsetting for the both of you, but the good news is that we caught this in time, and I have the proper treatments for Serena. And she will need a new diet." The doctor turned to Gia. "Are you still lactating?"

Gia nodded.

"Wonderful, so we'll get Serena fed today, and that will really help. I suggest feeding her right now, and then later on pumping and sending your breastmilk to the Langleys while Serena is with them."

"*While* she's with us?" Bronwyn repeated. "She's staying with us! She's not going anywhere! Isn't there something else we can feed her?"

The doctor grimaced. "Gia's breastmilk really is the best thing to keep Serena strong and healthy. But I will give you a recipe for seamilk. You make it from the extract of Padina Pavonica. It's a nutrient-packed algae that grows in the warm, shallow waters of the Mediterranean. It's really good."

The doctor scooped up Serena and passed her to Gia. Serena opened her baby blues to peer up at her mother. Though they looked dull, Serena's eyes still reminded her of Cameron. Gia sighed and held the baby close to her, breathing in her scent. Serena smelled sweet, like rosemary wafting in an ocean breeze. There was also a faint hint of dish soap, and Gia imagined that the odor lingered from Serena's time spent floating in the Langley's kitchen sink.

Gia untied her wrap dress and let the sleeves fall and then unfastened her bra, exposing her chest. At that moment, everything faded away, and it was just she and Serena, sitting on a stool together. No problems. No threats. Nothing but the love a mother has for a daughter. As the baby drank from her, Gia held Serena's little head in place. Gia closed her eyes and thought of her own mother and wished so much that she was there in the room instead of Bronwyn.

17

September 16th

If Queen Zale was making moves and forming alliances, then Queen Awa knew that she had no choice but to pursue that path as well. Therefore, the purpose of her trip to Brazil was two-fold. First, she would use the opportunity to check in on Gia's Rio de Janeiro beach club, Yemaya. Second, she planned to pursue a little diplomatic action, by way of a sly *rendezvous* with the leader of the Brazilian mermaids.

Christ the Redeemer cast his beatific gaze over the green valley of Rio. The statue, with its famous open arms, wasn't just a tourist attraction, it was also a landmark for the Mermaid world. Deep inside Mount Corcovado, a rocky passage led to a fast-moving stream. The rolling water, should one follow it, would lead you into the earth, under the Lagoa Rodrigo de Freitas, funneling you right into the ruins of the Brazilian mermaid colony. Three hundred fathoms below Ipanema—about the length of six soccer fields—stands the abandoned castle where the mermaids once lived. The stone labyrinth now served only as a governmental function—a meeting place for official business. The Brazilians—the Sugarloaves, as they called themselves—had long ago jettisoned their aquatic underworld for a sunnier existence by the beach.

The Sugarloaves, without a doubt, were the colony most adapted to life in the open air. They'd bought and developed large swathes of real estate all over Brazil, a large concentration of which was situated along the coastline of Rio.

Little did Gia know, however, that the Sugarloaves had been partying at Yemaya since it opened. So, when the President of the colony swished into the main palapa of the beach bar, he took a seat at his favorite table, which boasted a marvelous view of both Ipanema Beach and its intricately patterned cobble boardwalk.

Queen Awa spotted him from afar. Short and unassuming, he wasn't someone that most people would notice at first glance. He always dressed simply and his dark brown skin blended in with the camel-colored hues of his bowling-style button-down.

"João," Awa said, grazing her hand across his shoulder from behind, "how have you been?" After a quick embrace, Awa perched on a tall barstool across the high-top table from him.

"I am rich, and I am old. How are you, beautiful Queen Awa?"

"Ah, João, you know me. A queen never tires."

"And is your wife here?"

"She's back in Senegal at the moment, keeping an eye on Moussa."

"I am so sorry to hear the news about the passing of Oumar. Forgive me for not reaching out. Queen Zale has made everything rather difficult these days. A simple phone call feels like a declaration of war."

"I see. So, it must be quite scandalous for you to sit here with me in person. How does it feel having Old Zale run your life for you?"

"Certainly no one will ever tell me where I can drink a caipirinha in peace."

"Then, by all means, let's have a cocktail. We have much to discuss."

18

September 16th

Gia strutted into The Odeon wearing creamy over-the-knee vegan leather boots. Her mini dress was covered with oversized, opalescent palettes. The white cat-eye liner and teased up hair completed her 1960s-inspired ensemble. She felt sexy, but also terribly overdressed for a first date—even though it was technically a fake date, arranged by her publicist.

The French-by-way-of-Philly diner's windows overlooked West Broadway. The sidewalk was thick with photographers, influencers, and fans, all eyeing Gia, capturing her every move. Gia's security team flanked her and then moved out of the way, as she slid into a booth that faced the street.

Rising film star Riley Rose was already there, waiting for Gia.

"Hey," she whispered in an Australian accent, "I know this is intimidating at first, but I promise we'll finish dinner quickly and get out of here." Riley grinned and took a sip from a skinny highball glass.

"*Ciao*," Gia said, scooting over to Riley, "what are you drinking?"

"It's their house cocktail. Tequila. Here, try it." Riley pushed the drink toward Gia.

Gia wrapped her lips around the paper straw and sucked. "That is delicious."

"Mmm. So are you." Riley then burst out into hearty laughter. "I promise I'm not actually that cheesy. I just... wow... you look incredible."

"I am not allowed to wear my own clothes anymore."

"Tell me about it," Riley said, easing into the back of the banquette. Gia drank in the movie star's androgenous vibe. Riley's hair was cut short, shaved on the side, and styled into a rockabilly curve that cast a shadow across her angular face. Her amber eyes were smudged with dark liner. She wore a backless button-up, and since the shirt was also sleeveless, it showed off Riley's arms, which were covered in tattoos.

Gia ordered the same cocktail as Riley and tore off a piece of a baguette.

Riley stared down at Gia's plate and remarked, "It's been forever since I've witnessed anyone eat bread."

"This, Riley, is a tragedy. How is one able to live without bread—or pasta?"

Riley shook her head, smiling. "It's a poor quality of life, I'll give you that. But the fucking camera is unforgiving."

Gia frowned and thought, *America's unending obsession with diets is making the world sick.*

"Tell me all about you, Gia." Riley brushed Gia's hair off her shoulder and whispered to her again, "It's a good idea if we can get some shots of us really close like this. The press just loves that. Lower your head a bit and smile with your lips closed."

Gia did as instructed.

"That's perfect," Riley crooned, before returning her back to the banquette. "So, damn, you're a real-life mermaid, huh?"

Riley's question annoyed Gia very much, and she pulled away.

"Woah, woah," Riley said, hovering her hands above the table.

"We don't have to go there. Is there something else you want to talk about?"

Gia crossed her arms over her chest.

"Gia," Riley spoke in hushed tones, "that's really bad body language. It's not going to play well on camera. We need to look like we're connecting. It will be better for both of us, I promise. Please, drop your arms and let me get closer to you again. You can trust me."

Trust you? Gia scoffed in her mind. She narrowed her eyes at Riley. *Only untrustworthy people assured others of their trustworthiness.* Gia knew this because she'd deployed that line herself—many, many times before.

19

September 17th

"Yesterday's events at the Manhattan Animal Emergency Hospital were not only shocking, they were devastating on a personal level." On camera and through gritted teeth, Ashley Mason spoke to the OTN audience. "The assault I experienced by that Internet troll, Wishy-Washy... that *is* liberal America for you right there. My father is a hard-working man, an electrician, and he and my mother toiled for long hours in their blue collar jobs to send me to college. They're salt of the earth, and the accusation that he's somehow involved in a white nationalist organization is ludicrous."

Ashley rose from behind the anchor desk, and the jib followed her. "But let's address the other controversy from yesterday. And that's Gia Acquaviva. I have a very special guest here with me today."

She walked to a separate part of the studio that was dressed with two chairs and a bassinet. "I want to welcome Bronwyn Elizabeth Merritt Langley, President of our network."

Bronwyn swayed onto the set, seeming to teeter precariously on her high heels. She carried a swaddled Serena in her arms. Ashley rushed over to help Bronwyn into her seat, holding her up around the arms.

"You poor thing," Ashley cooed, "this whole mess with Murder Mermaid must be taking its toll on you."

"It really is Ashley."

"Who are ya holdin' there, Mrs. Langley?"

Bronwyn cracked a smile and looked down at Serena. "This is my grandbaby."

"Can I hold her?"

"Of course!" Bronwyn removed the swaddle and passed Serena to Ashley. Although Serena's tail had not fully recovered and regained all of its golden luster, she was on the mend and particularly animated that day.

"Oh my goodness," Ashley baby-talked, "you are just the most precious wittle thing I ever have seen." She held Serena up, bouncing her in the air. The baby's tail kicked side to side. "Look at this strong wittle lady."

A staffer walked on set with a baby bottle and Ashley handed Serena back to Bronwyn. "Pardon me," Bronwyn said, "it's dinnertime."

"By all means, please go ahead."

Bronwyn cradled Serena and tipped up the bottle. The baby took it and raised her hand to touch her grandmother's chin.

"That's just darling," Ashley sighed. "If you don't mind, could you tell me… what is she drinking?"

"This is seamilk, a special recipe. You see, we have a new doctor helping us care for Serena."

"Oh, really? Who is that?"

"Believe it or not, she's an NYU-trained OBGYN who also happens to be a mermaid."

"No!"

"In fact," Bronwyn gestured at a screen behind them. "I have a photo of her taken during her med school days here in New York." Dr. Kupolou's face appeared on cue.

However, Bronwyn had no idea what the consequences of her flippant disregard for the doctor's privacy would be—nor did she know that there would be no returning to the colony in Greece for Dr. Kupolou now.

20

September 1995

Florent had spent most of August in Venice. When he wasn't drinking in his suite at the Hotel Bauman, he would roam the streets, searching for Gia. He'd gambled in Gia's casino, never really spending a significant amount of money, merely enough so that he could loiter without disturbance. The air in Venice during that month had been mucky and oppressive, with throngs of tourists stomping through the twisty streets and over delicate bridges. The whole place felt like a sweaty armpit. And worst of all for Florent, Gia never showed up.

In early September, Florent made his way to Geneva to begin university. He rented very comfortable accommodations in the city's Old Town neighborhood and set about shopping to put his stamp on the apartment. Though Gia was ever-present in his mind, he resolved to focus on his studies. After all, that's what his father would have wanted, and he was of no mind to disappoint his old man, even in death. He hoped that it could be considered some form of redemption for what he had done.

Florent did his best to appear engaged and enthusiastic at orientation. He had chosen business school and planned to focus his studies on scientific innovation. A real chip off the old block. There was immense opportunity at school if he could just focus and make friends. After all, the sons and daughters of Europe's titans of industry were his classmates.

As he took a seat in his first Economics class, he noticed a few girls chatting in Italian as they entered the classroom. One of them caught his attention. She was deliciously curvaceous with long hair, so dark it was almost black. She raised her head, and when she did, Florent immediately noticed her almond eyes.

She looks so much like Gia.

His heart was pumping fast, and he wanted to jump out of his seat and take a place next to her, but the professor was already beginning the lecture.

This is good, very good.

He smiled for the first time since before his father died.

I will make that girl mine.

* * *

RATHER THAN POUNCING on the object of his affection right away, he decided that a better course of action would be to surveil this new girl and glean important information about how he might seduce her.

He discovered that her name was Louisa Peretti, and she was studying business, with a concentration in management. Should she excel in her classes with top marks, her parents had promised her that a mid-level job would be waiting for her in the family business in Milan. So, even though Louisa was tempted to party and hit the discos, she made a very conscious effort to keep her nose in her books. Florent realized that the best way to get to her was to volunteer to be her study buddy.

After a few weeks of positioning himself at varied locations both on and off-campus—where she would be certain to clock him studying—he finally approached her as she sat alone in a coffee shop, poring over her Economics book.

"*Ciao*," he said, interrupting her.

She looked up at him and replied in French, "*Bonjour*."

"I've seen you around school. We're in the same Economics class."

"Ah, yes. I was wondering when you would approach me. After seeing you everywhere that I have been, I imagined you might be following me."

He felt a light sting in her words, but he recovered quickly.

"Do you blame me? It's not as though I can buy you a drink in a bar. You never go out."

"True."

"May I sit?" he asked, gesturing toward the empty seat across from her.

She nodded.

"My master plan," he explained, "was to sidle up to you and weasel my way into getting you to study with me."

"My God, how boring."

"I agree. You're much too beautiful for that. I have, therefore, abandoned that plan and now wish to get straight to the point. I would like to buy you dinner, drink a bottle of wine together, and then make love to you at my apartment."

A blush crept up her neck and found a home on her face. "And I thought Italian men were forward."

"I love seeing your face flushed like this. Let's see if I can keep it like that."

21

September 18th

Dr. Kupolou's husband and twin daughters knocked three times on the doors of the Greek colony's Salt Cathedral, just as Gia had before her own trial. The large wooden doors creaked open, and Queen Zale glared at them as they descended the aisle toward her. Her long silver hair was loose and floated around her zaftig body like a curtain of snakes.

Normally, a trial of this sort required the presence of the Pan-Atargatic Council. But ever since Queen Zale had suspended the treaty, protocols were murky, seemingly being crafted on the fly.

"Sit," she commanded the family. They cowered, crumpling into a pew. Queen Zale closed her golden eyes and took in an enormous breath, raising her hands above her head. "O Gracious Tides bless the Nations of Atargatis, we are few."

The man and his two little girls hung their heads and repeated the prayer, "O Gracious Tides bless the Nations of Atargatis, we are few."

"The Gracious Tides are speaking now," Queen Zale said, angling her head, so that her hair fell backward off her ear. "Listen."

At first they only heard clicking sounds, like shells on a wind-chime bumping against one another in the breeze. Then, air rustled, soft as the ocean's zephyr, tickling their ears. From the wind came a multitude of whispers in Atargatis. "We are creation. Tides eternal ebb and flow. The clay withers against our sacred strength. Children of the sea, we shelter you no more. The oceans are rising again, reclaiming... reclaiming... reclaiming..."

The wind intensified suddenly inside the temple. In response, the queen began to levitate.

"O Gracious Tides," Queen Zale demanded, her voice booming over the rushing air, "ruler of the moon, cleanse these children, fill them with your storm!"

The breath of the ocean seized the family, elevating them and holding them like puppets in mid-air. The cyclone spun and spun. The girls screamed first, stretching wide their tiny mouths. Water poured in, distorting their lips, distending their cheeks.

Their father could only bear witness to this rush of seawater as it filled up his daughters, ripping them apart. He tried to reach for them, sought to protect them, but water battered his eyes and raced inside his lungs, choking him from the inside. The pain was unbearable, but it didn't last long. Just as suddenly as the storm began, it subsided, and the father and his daughters were dumped against the salt floor. He was breathing—but barely. The young girls were not. Their lifeless bodies laid still and pale.

Queen Zale summoned her servants. "Take this man ashore. Abandon him to the sand and the clay. He and his people have no place here."

22

September 20th

Above the pungent green waters of the Gowanus Canal loomed the ADET headquarters. The grey building had previously served as a warehouse but was now emblazoned with graffiti, featuring choice phrases such as: "Eat the Rich, Not Animals," "Fur Is Dead," and "Meat Is Murder."

Gia and her entourage graced the front door shortly after ten o'clock in the morning. Talia pressed the buzzer and ADET's purple-haired Senior Director of Engagement let them in.

"You must be Lee," Talia beamed, "I'm a huge supporter of the org and *super* excited to be here. Seriously, thank you so much for having us."

"Yeah, for sure, come on up," Lee replied, holding the metal door open. The stairwell was lit with blacklights and painted with the face of a giant, growling tiger.

Gia clacked up five flights of stairs to the main office on the top floor. The walls were covered with posters of celebrities holding dead, skinned animals—a lynx, a goose, whatever. Natural light streamed in from several plate glass windows, a big relief to Gia, who found the atmosphere dark and oppressive.

Talia, *La Nonna*, Gia, and Lee sat down on couches covered with upcycled jeans.

"First of all," Talia began, "like, *wow*, the attention and awareness ADET has been bringing to Gia's daughter is astounding."

"That's the power of direct action," Lee explained.

"Totes! So, we're here today because I want to propose a sort of partnership."

"I figured," Lee shrugged. "It's not often that billionaires pop by."

"Mkay, so, I've already inked a deal with Washi-Washi to help with amplification."

"Hmm. That's gonna be a no-go for us."

"Wait, what now? Washi-Washi is a no-go?"

"He wears fur all the time."

"Well, what if he goes vegan and does, like, a whole series of funny Klik Klak videos for ADET where he cooks vegan food... or.. I don't know... like shoots red paint at people out of a squirt gun."

"We're not really interested in virtue signaling. We are thinking Big Picture and investing our time in longer lasting partnerships."

"What about a three-year deal with Washi-Washi? I think that could be really big for ADET."

"We'll think about it."

"Turning our attention to Gia..." Talia patted her client on the knee. "She's really in need of help."

"We get that. It's why we've taken to the street on Gia's behalf. The Langleys should not be raising her baby. It's not right."

Gia opened her mouth to speak, but Talia cut her off. "Mkay, so I'm thinking we do like a big protest in Times Square, you know? To bring in even more eyeballs. What if we partner with some climate change orgs and clean up the ocean people and put Gia at the center. We could do a *'tail unveiling'* in a big water tank."

"Pardon me," Gia interjected, finally butting in before Talia's plans got out of hand, "I find this repulsive. I will not be treated as a spectacle and confined in that way. I am not an animal in a zoo." Her thoughts naturally turned to her experience with Q and she shivered involuntarily.

"For real!" Lee agreed. "That's probably super triggering for her, considering she was rescued from a *fucking aquarium* not that long ago. We obviously all saw the footage. That's a terrible idea, Talia—just awful, seriously. ADET would never get behind that. We're about protecting animals, not humiliating them."

"You are not listening to me!" Gia screeched. "What did I just say? I am *not* an animal!"

"Obvi, we know that, babe," Talia placated Gia, before going in on Lee. "Uh, Lee... hello, have you looked at your walls recently? Do the grotesque animals in your posters look like religious iconography? No, they sure don't. So, like, I'm not here for a lecture. TBH, I'm offering ADET the chance to get a lot of mainstream buy-in, and that's gonna bring in so much *dinero*. Imagine all the cow farms you guys can take down. You're gonna have, like, *'fight Chick-fil-A'* money. And we *all* know those fuckers need to be challenged."

"Hmm." Lee crossed their fingers and tapped their lips, deep in thought. "Look, we're not above a compromise. While we cannot do the Times Square dunk tank, ADET would not be opposed to a tasteful photoshoot featuring Gia and her beautiful tail."

23

November 1995

Louisa spoke nearly perfect French, which was excellent, because Florent's Italian was terrible. They had spent practically all their time together in the last few months. She was madly in love with the handsome Frenchman as he felt much more grown up to her than the other boys at the university. For his part, Florent considered her a nice distraction, but his mind never wandered far from thoughts of Gia.

As the couple left the cinema, Louisa remarked in French, "What a shocking ending. Do you think so?"

"You didn't see it coming?" Florent replied, casually.

"See it coming? That the killer would send Brad Pitt's wife's head to him in a box? No, that was not something I imagined would happen."

"The wife was simply too innocent, too naive." Florent shrugged his shoulders, seemingly unimpressed. "She had to die."

Louisa punched him in the arm and cursed at him, "*Stronzino!*"

"What does that mean?"

"It means you are a rude little piggy!"

He stopped in the middle of the street and grabbed his new girlfriend around the waist, jerking her toward him so her body collided forcefully with his. "Listen here, don't speak to me like that." Then he slid his hand up her back to the nape of her neck and tugged on her hair, leaning in to kiss her deeply.

She kissed him back, but when the kiss was over, she whispered. "I do not like it when you are so rough with me." Louisa placed her hands on his chest, pushing herself ever so slightly away from Florent.

"You'll get used to it." He felt rather pleased with himself. If he couldn't have Gia, Louisa was a malleable stand-in. Plus, he liked roughing Louisa up, because whenever he did, he thought of it as punishing Gia. And he wondered how violent Louisa might allow him to be with her. How far could he push things?

He took Louisa's hand and steered her toward his apartment.

When they made love that night, he took Louisa from behind. He buried his head into her long, dark hair, wishing she were Gia. And when he climaxed, it was Gia's face he conjured in his mind's eye.

24

September 25th

Gia gazed up at the silver skyscraper that was about to become her new home. It sliced into Manhattan's midtown bedrock like King Author's Sword—which is exactly why the developer had named the luxury highrise Excalibur. Truth be told, it wasn't just the metaphor that he liked; the builder was a closet fantasy nerd. Fetching nearly three hundred million dollars for the sale of just one of his forty-four units had merited him superstar status among his childhood friends, whom he still met with several times a year for a bit of incognito medieval cosplay.

But Gia wasn't in the market to buy, unfortunately. A year ago? Absolutely. Now, forget it. Her net worth had plummeted. The pieces of her hospitality portfolio that Q hadn't cleaned out or offloaded to his buddies were now under attack by her own kind.

Could she sell her plane? Most definitely.

Would she? Hell, no, not ever.

That plane was the only piece of freedom she had left, and no one was going to claw it away from her, no matter what.

So, renting was Gia's only solution... not that it was a particularly affordable option. The monthly lease on the two-floor Central-Park-facing condo Abby had snagged for her was a whopping one hundred and fifty-nine thousand dollars per month.

Alas, that was the cost of safety for Gia in the City That Never Sleeps, and she had no choice but to pony up the cash.

Abby led Gia and her security detail through the guarded, marble-encased private entrance and up to the fifty-seventh floor. At the front door of the apartment, Abby reached into her Celine bag and dug out a set of keys.

"All yours," she said, passing the key ring to Gia.

Gia unlocked the door and stepped into a red-lacquered foyer, pausing to lay her purse down on a bench. She passed into the sun-drenched living room. Seven floor-to-ceiling windows revealed a stunning view of Central Park. From this height, the carpet of green in front of her resembled a small lawn. Everything was dwarfed by the expanse of blue sky. Even the surrounding buildings looked like little Lego dwellings.

"Well?" Abby needled, fishing for a compliment.

"*Bellissima*," Gia replied. "You have found me exactly what I asked."

Abby licked the tip of her pointer finger and drew out an invisible checkmark in the air. "Abby Singer does it again!"

A few minutes later, Abby bid farewell, and Gia wandered through the immaculate apartment. The finishings were of the highest quality, expertly installed by skilled craftsmen. Rather than elation or gratitude, though, Gia felt a different emotion in the pit of her stomach.

This wasn't home.

It wasn't Venice or even London for that matter. She ached to be reunited with Serena, take her somewhere safe, and disappear into the darkness.

She could not help but long for her former anonymity.

Gia sunk into her new bed in the master suite. Her personal items were being packed up and brought over from the hotel via white-glove service. She wanted nothing more than to relish in this much-needed moment of solitude.

Unfortunately, there is no rest for the wicked, and just as soon as Gia had begun to unwind, her phone rang. A video call. She swiped to answer.

"*Methusalamme*!" she shrieked. "I have been waiting so long to hear your voice."

"Ah, *tesoro mio*," Vittore replied, "*La Nonna* would not allow me to call you until it was safe."

"Are you with Uncle Stavros?"

He chuckled and lowered his voice to a whisper, which, due to his faulty hearing, was still quite loud. "He follows me everywhere! He worries about me constantly. 'My young lover, do not fall... my young lover, eat this baklava...' and so on and so on! Bah! I tell him, 'Listen to me, you old fish! I have lived more than eighty years of my life without you! I can manage another five or so.' He crowds me like a mamma."

"But, Vittore, he loves you. I, for one, am so very happy that you have someone to take care of you in your golden years."

"Golden?! *Tesoro mio*, no, no. I am very tarnished by now. I am more like a bent and rusty old spoon. Nothing golden about me." In the background, she heard footsteps. "He comes!"

Uncle Stavros walked up to Vittore and gave him a kiss on the cheek. Vittore scrunched up his face and hissed.

"Tut tut!" Stavros clicked his tongue. "You must be grumpy because you are hungry!"

"No more food! You will have to roll me back to Venice!"

"Give me the phone, my young lover. I must speak with Gia."

Vittore grunted and sat back into his chair.

"I have very disturbing news from the colony here, Gia. The doctor who has been helping you... her husband was excommunicated. And Queen Zale murdered their twin daughters."

Gia recoiled. "Murdered them?"

"Yes, a week ago... after the doctor was seen on American television. Queen Zale is becoming unglued. We must do something."

Gia felt her pulse quicken before she remembered that she, too, had a queen in play on the board.

"Queen Awa has been making moves. She may have a solution. I will put a call in to her today to strategize."

25

October 1st

"Harper," Talia snapped, "I don't like being kept waiting."

Sauntering into her dressing room, Harper shrugged off her blazer. "Have you noticed that you're at *my* place of work?"

"How could I not? I've been, like, on the lookout for Nazi flags."

"Oh, for God's sake, Talia. Don't be so dramatic. It's hardly 1930s Germany over here. Goldie Stern runs the network. He's also Jewish, remember?"

"Barely! He probably took his *Bar Mitzvah* money and never returned to synagogue, ever again! Can you blame me for being nervous around here? Anyways... lemme get to the point."

"Please do." Harper collapsed onto the sofa.

Talia's eyes gleamed. "I come to you with a very exciting proposal."

Harper rested her palms on her temples and squeezed her face backward. *This woman is fucking insufferable!*

Talia continued, "Obvi, everyone who knows anything about TV knows that you're flailing over here at best... and *failing* at wor—"

"Listen, bitch—"

"Hold on, for fuck's sake! I am a bitch, mkay? Loud and proud. So, let a bitch talk! I have a scoop for you. Actually, let me put this another way. Like, not only do I have one scoop for you. I've got the biggest, most fatty ice cream sundae ever... more scoops than you can imagine. You know, like, when restaurants make thousand-dollar gold-covered ice cream? That's what I'm about to serve you... on a motherfucking platter."

"Okay."

"*Okay*?! Are you not hearing what I'm saying? I have information that's going to catapult you into the goddamn stratosphere, and you're over here, like, 'Uh, whatever' about it."

"Were you a loser in high school, Talia? Did you get blackballed from a sorority? What is it? Something has obviously happened to you to make you..." Harper looked her up and down, "*like this*."

Talia ignored the insult and continued trying to thrash out a deal. "I know what you want. I can get it for you. Daytime TV. Talk show."

Harper exploded into laughter. "Sure."

Talia locked eyes with Harper, hooking into her soul like a tow truck pulling a VW Bug. "Your coverage in Sicily was *very good*. There's no denying that. You found Gia. You exposed that mafia guy. You got coverage of those other mermaids. You uncovered a lot. But there's much more. So much more that you don't know. There are other mermaids out there, Harper. Like tons. High profile ones. I have an inside source giving me all kinds of shocking information. What I'm offering you is the key to unlock that treasure chest. It'll be open season on mermaids, and you'll be the only one with a rifle. All that I'm asking in return is positive coverage of Gia."

26

October 3rd

The second Gia's heel hit the red carpet, she thought of Nico. He had told her many times how much he hated being famous, and now she understood why.

"Gia," a reporter said, shoving a microphone in her face, "who are you wearing?"

"Vintage Mugler."

The man squealed. "No! Twirl, we must see a twirl."

She flashed a fake smile and said, "*Amore*, I would love to, but I am very afraid to fall and tear this dress. I must return it to the archives spotless."

The heavily pleated white silk gown swayed with her as she cut in front of other celebrities, gliding toward her target. Closing the space between her and Riley Rose, she found her date for the evening, making love to the camera. Riley's shrunken velvet tuxedo was paired with extremely high stilettos.

"*Ciao*," Gia strode up to Riley and kissed her on the cheek. The paparazzi went wild and began screaming both their names, demanding that they kiss.

Riley leaned over and whispered to Gia, "You're getting better at this, aren't you? Why don't we feed the hungry trolls?"

Gia nodded. Riley tilted Gia's head back and gave her the most perfect, most elegant, most photogenic kiss in history. Riley knew their photos would be all over social media within fifteen minutes—and all over the world within hours.

There was no need for additional time working the red carpet. The pair had done their job with the press. Riley took Gia's hand and disappeared behind the step and repeat.

"Can we have a do-over of that kiss?" Riley asked. "Only, let's make it real this time."

Gia gazed into Riley's eyes. They were the color of the Grand Canyon, with flecks of green. Gia experienced an odd sensation when she locked eyes with Riley: it was the feeling of being suspended over the Canyon, walking along a tightrope. If she let herself fall, what would happen?

* * *

THE STAGE inside the Manhattan nightclub Extra Large was crammed with drag queens. It was Queer Media's biggest night of the year, and all the stars were out. The event was being hosted by Mama Lu, the top drag performer in the world.

Mama Lu cupped her hands above her eyes, peering out into the audience. "So many interesting people here tonight!" she buzzed. "Girls..." she said, turning to her drag babies, "do you smell something strange?"

"Lu," one queen shouted, "I do! There *is* a weird smell in the air."

Mama Lu opened her nostrils and trotted along the stage, smelling the audience. "It smells like... like fish!"

Another queen, a famous transgender star, stepped out in front and said, ever so demurely, "Oh, Lu, that's just me." She fanned her hands in front of her nether regions.

"No!" Mama Lu bellowed. "It's something else. Wait! Is that... do I see a *mermaid* in the audience tonight?"

At their cocktail table in the center of the audience, Riley burst out laughing, but Gia was mortified and she felt heat rising to find a home on her face.

"Miss Gia Acquaviva," Mama Lu sang, "come up to the stage, darling."

The spotlight wobbled its way around the room and finally landed on Gia. The audience hooted and clapped. A chant broke out. "Gia... Gia... Gia!"

Riley cocked her head to the side. She rose and walked into the spotlight, holding out her hand, "Gia, love, when Mama Lu calls, you answer."

Riley escorted Gia through the audience, ensuring her date didn't trip. The whole way, the spotlight followed her like a heat-seeking missile. At the steps of the stage, Riley bent down on one knee, and dramatically waved her arm open, showing Gia off to Mama Lu.

"Oh, my!" Mama Lu fanned herself. "How galant! Come, Gia, here, stand next to Mama Lu."

Gia inched her way toward the drag legend.

"Don't look so petrified!" Mama Lu chided Gia. "I don't bite... well, maybe only a little." When Gia was finally beside her, Mama Lu took her hand. "A pretty thing you are. And tell me, are you here with Riley Rose tonight?"

Gia shook her head, yes.

"Riley..." Mama Lu hummed in a high vibrato, "I guess this means you eat sushi?"

Riley broke out into hysterics. "Only with a little wasabi," she yelled back.

Mama Lu moved Gia to center stage. "Gia," she said, "we have a tasty treat for you tonight!"

The drag queens parted like Rockettes, and two buff, shirtless men carried a throne onto the stage. The chair sat positioned inside an enormous clamshell. Mama Lu installed Gia on the throne, and then the muscle men lifted her up onto their shoulders. The band started playing a calypso tune, and Mama Lu began singing, "Under the Sea" from "The Little Mermaid."

Gia did her best to control the expression on her face, but nevertheless, she could feel her cheeks blazing. She had never felt more humiliated in her life.

27

October 8th

Bronwyn warmed some of Gia's breastmilk in a pan and squeezed a dropper, stirring in a small dose of the hormone Dr. Kupolou had formulated for Serena. She hummed her favorite song as she contemplated the tincture in front of her. Her grandbaby had been such an angel for the past few weeks. Serena had been recovering beautifully.

Royce had set up the doctor with personal and professional space in the house and had flown her husband over from Greece—he was apparently a refugee of some sort, but neither would explain to the Langleys what had happened. They seemed terrified, traumatized. But why? Bronwyn and Royce didn't know.

Regardless, and even though it was the Langley's fault that the good doctor was in this predicament, Royce and Bronwyn had swooped in before Gia and *La Nonna* were able to, ensconcing the doctor in a private wing at Langley Manor, offering up their extensive resources for her every need.

Now, with Gia's staff sending fresh breastmilk every other day and the baby so happy, Bronwyn was beginning to feel terribly comfortable and blissfully at ease.

She prepped a bottle for Serena and then held her between her arms and the overstuffed feeding pillow in her lap. The baby kicked her legs.

What a joy. Her little legs had returned, thanks to the hormone.

When they first came back, they looked like matchsticks, but they were beginning to fill out again.

While Serena sucked from the bottle, Bronwyn flipped on the wall of TVs in her office. Ashley Mason was on OTN. Just to the left, there was Harper, broadcasting live on LION.

When a photo of Serena popped up on screen, Bronwyn's interest was piqued and she unmuted Ashley.

"Couldn't you just *die*?" Ashley said. "We were sent this picture of The Little Mermaid from the Langleys just this morning. As you can see, the little baby's feeling strong and doing just great!"

Suddenly, the ticker tape at the bottom of the screen that was tuned to LION caught Bronwyn's eye.

BREAKING NEWS: Silicon Valley execs exposed as mermaids.

Bronwyn turned on the sound, to listen to Harper's reporting.

Harper read from the teleprompter with gusto. "The Dean Brothers have been the toast of Big Data for almost a decade. Bryce Dean and his younger brother, Kyle, started their firm after years of hopping around top tech companies. Their net worth is estimated to be more than two hundred million dollars. But today, they're not making the news because of some technological breakthrough or even because of a breach due to hacking. What I have to tell you about the Dean Brothers might be shocking to hear. It was for me. They are *mermaids*."

To the side of Harper, an image appeared of Bryce and Kyle hanging their tails off a boat. "This photo was taken in sunny Southern California. Notice their bright green tails. That's not makeup. It's not a costume. This isn't photoshopped. This is a real photo of two mermaids. Wait... do I still call them mermaids? Mermen? Merpeople? Who knows!

There's something fishy going on here… something conspiratorial. Let's put some pieces together. Two mermen control Silicon Valley. Gia controls a global network of casinos and clubs. These merfolks all seem incredibly wealthy. Is there a *vast global conspiracy* of merfolk plotting to take down humankind? We'll figure it out together. Stay tuned for—"

Bronwyn flicked off the TVs, shaking her head. She shivered. *It makes sense, of course, that there are more mermaids. There's Gia, the doctor… the ones Harper caught on tape recusing Gia. How many are out there?*

28

October 10th

"This is an international crisis, João," the Prime Minister of Belize, Pablo del Rio Dulce, insisted.

Indeed, in the mermaid world, there was a growing fracture. President João had used his close relationship with the colony in Belize to convince the Prime Minister and a small group of delegates to come to Rio. Queen Awa had pulled a similar diplomatic sleight of hand with the mermaids from the Arctic Circle.

Awa very much hoped all the leaders would join an alliance against Zale and the Californians.

"What exactly is the plan, Queen Awa?" the Belizean Prime Minister demanded. "What is the goal of outing our own flesh and blood? Not since ancient times have Mermaids lived out in the open. And with good reason!"

The three delegates from the Arctic Circle observed the interactions without speaking. Their translucent skin glittered with the illuminated light reflected from the palace's many lanterns. Having had the least exposure to conditions above the water, the Arctic Ice Folk, as they were called, maintained a strange, aquatic beauty and sported visible gills. If this had been a Marvel movie, the actors playing the Ice Folk would most likely have been required to arrive at the studio lot early in the morning to apply prosthetics and special effects makeup.

Within the mermaid community, it had been theorized that all Mermaid life could be traced back to the Arctic Circle. For that reason, the colony was highly influential. In the past century, however, the Greek mermaids had consolidated power and wealth, raising up Queen Zale as the de facto leader of the Pan-Atargatic nations.

Queen Awa lifted a finger, drawing the room's eyes in her direction. "Mankind is brutal. There is no mistaking that. The never-ending wars, the subjection within their own races... a seeming inability to find commonalities and build lasting alliances. But I ask you this... how can we stand by as Queen Zale murders innocent children in front of their parents? If we do not take a stand against the Greeks, then we are sending a message to Zale that this behavior is acceptable. Do you find it acceptable?"

Awa looked around the room at the other leaders, awaiting their reaction. Everyone was silent, and appeared to be deep in thought. She realized she had more persuading to do. So, she steered the conversation into a hot topic that she was sure would stir them up.

"Let us also focus our minds on the greater risk: our own survival. Mankind has so polluted the oceans—the true lungs of the planet—that in fifty or a hundred years, maybe less, the waters we call home may be uninhabitable."

"Exactly!" The Prime Minister slammed his hand down on the stone table.

Queen Awa had hooked him, and she continued on, seemingly more impassioned than before. "I have observed much during my reign. I have interacted with Man, and have come to understand them. But we are limiting ourselves as well as our power by swimming below the surface. By bringing the truth about us out into the bright sunlight, we can give a voice to the sea. We can manipulate Man to do as *we* please. Though the Atargatic nations are few, so many of our kind have lived among Man and achieved greatness. The tides are rising. It is time for the children of the sea to rise as well."

"Queen Awa," one of the Ice Folk spoke in a low frequency, like the melting of ice on a warm day, "do you believe that the princes from California will join this crusade?"

"Eventually," she shrugged.

"And Queen Zale, the Ancient?" asked another of the Ice Folk.

"I fear for our future if we lay down our collective fates at the feet of Zale. Hear me when I say this... I have glimpsed into those golden eyes of hers and what I saw was only oblivion."

Awa paused to let the last bit land.

"We must force Zale's hand," Awa explained. "If we control the story and the flow of information, then we have the upper hand."

29

October 20th

On the ground below the jet, Gia scanned great swaths of farmland, all neatly cut geometric shapes in shades of green and yellow. Talia was droning on again, prepping Gia with talking points for what Talia called, "the tap-in tipping point."

Talia had landed Gia a much-coveted one-on-one interview with America's most beloved talk show host—and self-made billionaire—Opal Windspray.

Washi-Washi was in the back of the plane, taking selfies and quick snippet videos to post on Klik Klak. His role was to document the trip to Chicago and capture Gia's more intimate and private moments.

However, the louder the commotion became around Gia, the thicker and taller her walls became. The limelight suffocated her to the point of causing anxiety, and she wanted nothing more than to press an eject button connected to the seats of every unwanted guest on her jet, shooting them out into the sky and far, far away from her.

"Uh, helllllloooooo!" Talia waved her hand in front of Gia's face, snapping her fingers demandingly. "Are you listening? This is literally the biggest and most important day of your life, and I need your full attention."

Gia blinked her daydream away and returned, unfortunately, to reality.

"Have some respect, Talia. Do not snap your fingers in my face as if you are training a puppy. I am perfectly capable of focusing."

Talia groaned and got back to the business of training her unruly client.

* * *

WHEN THE AIR steps tumbled downward from the belly of the plane and Gia stepped out onto the tarmac, she could not have been more shocked to see who was leaning against an Escalade, waiting for the whole crew.

Gia whipped around to face Talia, "What is *she* doing here?"

"Harper is going to help us get the message out today."

"*Puttana*!" Gia said under her breath.

"Relax," Talia said, talking out of the side of her mouth. "It's all coming together. We've got Washi-Washi here for the queers, Gen Z, and the libs, and Harper's here for the grannies and gun-toting truck drivers. Honestly, it's, like, *really* annoying for you to constantly question my vision when my actual goal is only to help *you*." Talia picked up her speed, briskly approaching Harper to exchange a pair of air kisses.

"Hey, Gia," Harper crowed, a sickly sweet smile plastered on her face.

"*Buongiorno*."

The two women sized each other up. When it seemed that a light frost might cover the entire area, Talia pushed them both in the car.

* * *

Opal Windspray's studio occupied an entire block on Chicago's Miracle Mile. A producer kept Gia backstage while Opal filmed the first segment.

Washi-Washi's phone had been confiscated, but he had anticipated as much. There was no way he wasn't going to capture all the action, so to compensate for his missing phone, he was sporting a pair of vintage Google Glasses he'd bought online. They'd film everything and send it all to Klik Klak.

Harper sat next to him in the front row of the audience, thinking that she did not particularly enjoy facing the ass end of the camera.

It's fine, she mused, *that will all change in less than an hour.*

Opal spoke to her A camera, with her rich, deep voice. "My guest, Gia Acquaviva, has been the subject of global fascination for over a year. Siren, alleged murderess, doting mother, tabloid princess... we think we know her, but we have no idea. Today, Gia Acquaviva gets candid. For the first time ever, she will tell her story, unfiltered and unabridged, in her own words. Let's give a warm, Opal welcome to Giaaaaa Acquavivaaaaaaa!"

The producer tapped Gia on her shoulder. That was her cue. And Gia breezed onto the set.

No more holding back, Gia thought, gunning herself up, *today I take back control of my life.*

Gia projected a calm aura of total confidence. Her vibe was Angelina Jolie, pre-Brad Pitt, post-Billy Bob.

She embraced Opal and let the talk show host rock her back and forth in what was a characteristically exaggerated hug. Those cuddles —and the tears that often followed them—had garnered Opal dozens of daytime Emmys.

Gia nestled into Opal's famous yellow couch, and Opal dove right into things.

"Gia, welcome."

"Thank you, Opal."

"You've had quite the year. A real roller coaster."

Gia shrugged while smiling. "I would not disagree."

"How are you doing?" Opal asked, leaning in to pat Gia's knee. "Really? How is your *heart*?"

Gia hesitated, then batted her eyelashes, "It is still beating, thankfully."

Opal took in that response, and the B camera zoomed in to examine Opal's face, deep in thought.

"I can imagine that you aren't used to this kind of public scrutiny. Before the events with Nicolás Ángel Fernández, you lived a quiet life... although, admittedly, it was rather lavish!"

"Opal," Gia laughed, placing a demure expression on her face, "someone told me that you have two private planes, so, it seems that you are ahead of me there."

"Touché," Opal replied. "Before we talk about what happened with Nico... can you tell me a little bit about Cameron Langley and the child you share?"

Gia closed her eyes and inhaled deeply, speaking slowly, "Cameron was a beautiful soul. The love of my life. I have had no greater joy than bringing our baby into the world."

"Your daughter, Serena, whom the press has dubbed 'The Little Mermaid'."

Gia nodded, "I do not like when they call her that."

"Why?"

"Because I feel that it dehumanizes her."

"I see. And when did you last see Serena?"

Gia imagined shaking a champagne bottle inside her chest and popping the cork. The fizz burned, and she used that energy to force a tear out of the corner of one eye. "It has been too long, Opal. I am missing the special days of watching my baby grow up—something every mother cherishes. I have not been allowed to hold Serena or even *to see her* in over a month."

"You've filed a custody case alleging violation of the Hague Convention. Can you speak about that?"

"My lawyer has advised me not to... but I would like to ask all of you a question." Gia turned to face the audience, dabbing at her eye with a tissue. "Do you think it is right that a mother be kept from her newborn? Do you think it is fair, just, or logical that two people who have never spent one single day underwater should raise a baby mermaid?"

The audience groaned their collective displeasure.

Opal drew Gia's attention back to her. "Those are serious questions, and I want to dive into them. Can you tell me when you'll be allowed to see your daughter again?"

"Opal, do you know that they make me pump and send my breastmilk to her every other day? Sometimes being kept away from my daughter is more than I feel I can handle."

"Gia, tell me about Nico. You were facing charges for his murder in Venice, but they've since been dropped."

"I never hurt him. I have never hurt anyone. I am incapable of such monstrous acts. Do you know what I think? I believe that I am a victim of prejudice. Ever since Odysseus, mermaids have been portrayed as killers, luring sailors to their deaths. To me, this sounds very much like the same chauvinistic mindset that has kept women oppressed for thousands of years. Mermaids are not killers. We are kind creatures who prefer to keep to ourselves. Many people have crossed paths with mermaids without ever having known. After all, Opal, you should understand this very well, since *you yourself* are a mermaid."

"What?" Opal balked.

"Your father's father emigrated from Senegal to the United States. His passport gave an address in Dakar, but that was not the truth, was it? He actually came from the mermaid colony."

The audience whispered audibly to each other. Washi-Washi streamed it all online in a Klik Klak Live, which was amassing millions of viewers.

Harper's heart pumped furiously. Knowing that she had all the juice on Opal—and that she was going to squeeze it 'til the last drop—was the most exhilarating feeling. It seemed that her alliance with Gia had been the right move.

Opal shook her head violently, "This is preposterous!" She signaled to her producer, "Turn the cameras off!"

30

Christmas Eve 1995

Paris was bone-chilling cold. Florent shoved his hand into fur-lined gloves as he exited church, linking arms with both his mother and his girlfriend.

"It is wonderful to have you both here," Sophie beamed. "Louisa, I am surprised that your family did not want you to come home to Italy."

"They did, *Madame* Bisset," she replied. "But Florent is so persuasive, so when he explained to my mother that it would be his first Christmas without his father, she relented and allowed me to come to Paris to see you both."

"That is so kind of her." Sophie swallowed a lump in her throat. The truth was that she really missed Pierre. Even though they were divorced, that hadn't made her stop loving him. Also, Florent wasn't always the easiest child to deal with, so she missed having Pierre's help with parenting. She had observed Florent becoming more and more guarded and brittle. That worried her. However, it appeared to Sophie that Louisa helped to soften Florent's edges a bit. Nevertheless, her son vexxed her greatly.

Sophie, Florent, and Louisa turned a corner and entered Sophie's favorite brasserie on the Champs-Élysées. They were seated at a table next to the window. A very light dusting of snowfall began outside, barely more than flurries, but it made Louisa smile.

"How beautiful!" she squealed.

"*Magnifique*," Florent agreed.

Sophie ordered a bottle of wine. "Louisa," she said, "tell me about your family. What do they do?"

Florent jumped in for Louisa. "Her father is in the tire business."

"I was speaking to Louisa, Florent."

"Don't start, *Maman*."

"I am merely taking an interest in your friend, my son. The lady can speak for herself."

"But asking what her family does... how they make money... don't be so provincial, *Maman*."

Sophie snapped back at him, but she had lost Florent's attention. He was focused on something of much greater importance to him.

Across the street, strolling under the falling snow was Gia, leaning into the arms of a tall, muscular man.

He instinctively jumped up, his lap crashing against the table. He knocked it hard enough that the three glasses of wine fell over, spilling into their laps. He hardly noticed.

He tried to squeeze past Louisa and run after Gia, but his mother called him back.

"Florent!" Sophie yelled. "Get back here this instant! What has come over you? Do not be rude. Help us clean up this mess you made."

He relented and helped sop up the spilled wine. By the time he made it out the front door, Gia was gone. He ran two or three blocks anyway, searching for her.

He wondered if he had really seen her, or if she'd only been some kind of phantom vision. He hung his head and forced himself to trudge back toward the restaurant.

31

October 21st

"Opal Windspray is a mermaid," Harper said to the camera in the LION studio. "I could never have imagined those words falling from my lips. We are in unprecedented times. However, dear viewers, I want you to know that as these shocking stories come through, you are safe here with me. You have an inside seat on this Pirates of the Caribbean ride, because I am the captain of your ship. My personal relationship with Gia Acquaviva makes me privy to exclusive information. And who does that benefit? You! Because I would never hold back from telling you the truth."

Goldie had put Harper live on camera during every single hour of the past twenty-four. Harper hadn't slept at all, but she was running on pure adrenaline and ambition, and she felt more alive and energized than ever.

The network was experiencing its highest lifetime ratings, and Goldie was happy enough that he could have rolled his wheelchair down a half-pipe into a full flip.

"Tonight," Harper continued, smiling wide into the camera, "I have two surprise guests joining me via satellite. They are two of the most important individuals in the global underwater mermaid network. I am joined by... let me make sure I say these names right... Queen Awa Diop of Senegal and President João Cruz Oliveira of Brazil. Welcome to the show."

"Pleased to be here," Queen Awa replied, bowing her crowned head. Of course, Awa wasn't normally one for crowns, but this was a rather rare occasion. So, she'd pulled out her favorite one, which was fashioned from black and white pearls, arranged in a scalloped pattern.

"Happy to make your acquaintance, Miss Langley," João said.

"Queen Awa," Harper interjected, "let's start with you. Your face is already well known. You saved Gia when she was trapped in Quintilio Mosca's aquarium in Sicily. It was my team that caught you on tape. It was really such an incredible moment."

"Harper, injustice anywhere is a threat to justice everywhere. I am not a queen who sits idly by, watching my people suffer. I felt it was my duty as a leader within the Pan-Atargatic world to step in and help a mermaid who was in great distress."

"The Pan.. what is it?" Harper asked. "What did you say?"

"Pan-Atargatic. That is our coalition of mermaid nation-states."

Harper's eyes widened, "*Nation*-states?"

"Of course. What do you think? That mermaids live at the bottom of the sea in shipwrecks, guarding treasure chests? No. We have complex societies and well-developed political networks."

"Speaking of politics," Harper replied, turning her attention to João, "President João Cruz Oliveira... what do I call you, sir?"

"President João is fine, Miss Langley."

"You got it. So, President João, from my research, you are a real estate developer in Brazil. Is that right?"

"Among other things."

"What other things exactly?"

João leaned back.

Harper furrowed her brow. "President João?"

"I am not sure I feel comfortable answering that question."

"I see. Tell me, why have you come on the program tonight if you are unwilling to answer my questions?"

"Ahem," he swallowed a gulp of water before replying, "I am here as a show of support for my old friend, Queen Awa, and I am here to say that Brazil stands behind Gia Acquaviva."

Harper cocked her head to the side. "Have you met Gia?"

"Yes," he lied. "Special woman indeed. Very accomplished."

"Hmm." Harper decided not to press him on his response. "Queen Awa, back to you. During our pre-interview, you mentioned that you wanted to discuss a few of these high-profile mermaid outings that have been causing such a sensation as of late."

"I do, thank you. First, Opal... *Windspray*... this is not actually her last name. Her real name is Opal *Ndiaye*, and she is my great-grandniece by marriage."

"Opal is your *niece*?" Harper repeated. It wasn't so much a question as it was a knee-jerk reaction to shock.

The viewers must have dropped their popcorn by now, Harper marveled. This story was so much more complicated than she imagined.

Awa explained, "Opal's grandfather is the brother of my wife, Mariama. Mariama is the Queen Consort of Senegal. We personally waved goodbye to Mariama's brother when he left Dakar."

"Wait," Harper shook her head, trying to make sense of everything, "let's break this down step by step. First... you're gay?"

"I have yet to meet a truly heterosexual mermaid. In my colony 'gay' marriage... 'queer' marriage... whatever you want to call it... has been normal since the beginning of time."

"Incredible. And if Opal is your great-grandniece... sorry, Opal is over sixty years old... how is that possible? How old are you?"

"Shame on you. A lady never tells her age," Queen Awa smirked conspiratorially.

Harper ran some calculations in her head, "You have to be... what... more than a hundred and twenty years old?"

"Ah, much more than that."

"Oh, my God," Harper's mouth dropped, and she stared into the camera. "LION viewers, this is just as mind-blowing for me as it is for you. Let me pull myself together here. Mmm, this is a lot to process."

"Take your time, Harper," Awa said, adjusting the crown on her head.

"Is it true that you know the Dean Brothers?"

"And their mother, Queen Karen."

"Sorry, are you saying... Bryce and Kyle Dean are... *princes*?"

"Harper, if you are planning to repeat everything I say, we are going to be here for quite a long time."

"So Queen... Queen Karen... she's queen of what exactly?"

"California."

Harper burst into hysterical laughter. "Queen... of *California*?"

Awa wasn't laughing.

"My apologies," Harper stifled her giggles. "You have a message for Bryce and Kyle Dean, is that right?"

Awa nodded. "I do have something to say to those little boys."

Then she narrowed her eyes and spoke through gritted teeth.

"You two have fucked with the wrong queen."

32

November 1st

Talia rapped at Gia's bedroom door, "The reporter from *Vogue* is here."

"Give me ten minutes," Gia called out.

The public's appetite for everything mermaid was insatiable. Together *La Nonna*, Talia, Gia, and Queen Awa had cracked open the Pandora's box of the ocean, unleashing a fanatical fervor the likes of which the world had never seen. And, best of all, America was falling in love with Gia.

For example, that day alone, Talia had tripled booked Gia. First was this *Vogue* interview. Then there was a trip up the Hudson with River Watcher, an organization devoted to ending water pollution in the Hudson Valley. The day would wrap up with yet another staged date with Riley Rose.

With the passing of each day, Gia grew more adept at media manipulation.

Gia slipped into a cream-colored satin suit and a gauzy button-down, completing her ensemble with a pair of beige Mary Jane heels.

The next two hours were full of ass-kissing nonsense and softball questions, mostly of the sartorial nature, such as, "Do mermaids really wear shell bras?"

Gia smiled on cue, cried on cue, and even hugged on cue. Talia could not have been more pleased.

"Excellent work," Talia said, patting Gia on the back after the *Vogue* reporter departed.

"Please," Gia shrunk back, "do not touch me."

"Yeah, yeah... no worries, my bad."

Good God, Gia was such a natural star that she was even charming Talia.

"How long before the next appointment?" Gia inquired.

"We should leave in like an hour."

"I will be in my room."

Gia returned to her cocoon of privacy. These necessary but invasive exchanges left her feeling tired. She had to stay clear on her goal: to win Serena back.

She texted *La Nonna* from the burner phone.

Any news?

After a moment, *La Nonna* responded. *Judge will hold a press conference in Venice tomorrow.*

Gia sighed and clicked her teeth. *Not about Nico. I want to know about Serena.*

Instead of replying, *La Nonna* phoned.

"There is a reason I texted you and did not call," Gia snapped.

"Ah, yes, my sincere apologies, *Signorina* Acquaviva. How could I forget the antisocial portion of your antisocial personality disorder?"

"Now that you have gotten rid of Q, you have become quite comfortable, haven't you? Always making derisive little jokes."

"If we remember properly, *angioletta*, it was you, not me, who 'got rid' of *Signor* Mosca."

"Must I prompt you every time to just get on with it? I suppose I must. So, please, for fuck's sake, get on with it."

"*Madonna!*" *La Nonna* cursed to herself.

Gia groaned.

"Huntington has requested a hearing in New York state court on the 16th."

"State court?" Gia repeated. "Why?"

"A formality, a part of the process."

"Do we need to prepare?"

"Relax, *sirenetta*. Everything is under control."

La Nonna's words made Gia tense up. Usually when everything was under control, *La Nonna* did not feel the need to say so. She simply acted, and things were as they should be.

"When can I expect to be reunited with my daughter?"

"*Signorina* Acquaviva, you are doing everything right. Simply continue with your role... which is to massage the media... and allow me to get on with mine. Yes?"

* * *

GIA TIPPED the last drops of the bottle of red wine into her cup.

"Another bottle?" she asked Riley.

"Why not?"

"Are you going to continue drinking through a straw like a toddler?"

Riley tapped her straw against the rim of her glass. "At least it's a stainless steel straw. Can't ruin this million-dollar smile, babe."

In a way, Riley reminded Gia of both Nico and Cam. Riley had the goofy humor of Cameron and the smouldering sex appeal of Nico. Not a bad combination, really.

Gia flagged the waiter and made the order. Despite seeing each other for the past six weeks, the "relationship" between Gia and Riley hadn't really gone anywhere. The pair enjoyed great chemistry, but the high degree of public scrutiny curbed a lot of the appeal for Gia.

Men had always been so easy to manipulate. However, Gia had always chosen her lovers—and chosen well—but that was a luxury that she was not allowed in this arranged match.

Plus, there was something walled-off about Riley.

As if sensing Gia's trepidation, Riley leaned across the table. "I was thinking... you haven't seen my apartment. I would like to take you tonight. If you're up for it?"

Gia didn't answer right away. She took the chance to gaze deeply into Riley's eyes. They were like two fish hooks.

What would Riley use as bait?

33

November 1st

Bronwyn approved the tablescape, complimenting her housekeeper on a job well done. When she was alone in the dining room, she realized that time was slipping away.

"Darling," she pressed the "talk" button on the intercom, speaking to Royce, who was across the estate in their master closet, "are you dressed?"

He wrestled with his shoes. "Not quite," he grunted.

"Do you need help?"

"No, no," he made crunching sounds as he spoke.

"Royce!"

"Mmm?"

"Don't tell me you're eating candy!"

"I'm not," he replied, nearly choking on a Werther's Original hard caramel and pounding his chest to catch his breath.

"*Diabetes!*" Bronwyn whisper-shouted. "Not to mention, you'll ruin your dinner."

"I have never in my life, *not once*, ruined my dinner, my darling wife. Now, buzz off!" He then pressed the intercom's buzzer six or seven times, making each punch progressively longer, knowing that the noise would really tick Bronwyn off.

Bronwyn ignored him, and instead observed her reflection in the glass panels of the hutch. She sighed. *I don't even look like myself.* She studied her reflection for a beat longer. *Never mind that. Tonight isn't about looking pretty. It's about persuasion.*

For the evening's special dinner she had flown in a vegan sous-chef from a trendy L.A. restaurant to serve as second-in-command to their in-house chef. Along with the rest of the planet, Bronwyn had learned many things over the last few weeks, including that the mermaid diet was almost exclusively plant-based. The night's high-profile guests deserved only the best.

Royce trotted in, finally.

"You didn't bring the baby, Royce. Where is she?"

"What?"

"Darling, I want Serena at dinner. I told you to bring her down here from the crib. Don't you listen to anything I say?"

"Bronwyn, you say a lot of things. How the hell am I supposed to know what's important enough to listen to?"

There was no denying that relations were becoming more and more acrimonious between the couple. And Bronwyn had to admit that she missed the days when they were in lock-step.

"Royce," she put on her sweetest tone, "if it's not too much trouble, might you bring our granddaughter downstairs?"

He huffed and turned around, heading back up the main stairs.

From the back stairs of the house, she heard quiet footsteps.

"Good evening," she sang out, turning to face Dr. Kupolou and her husband. "Shall we go through to the library for a cocktail?"

There, they found the part-time butler, who had recently been brought on full-time, since there were new residents at the manor. He shook up and poured out a row of Manhattans.

The doctor's husband was a strange fellow, Bronwyn had decided. He'd barely spoken in the weeks that he and his wife had been at the Langleys'. An odd shock of white hair ran down the middle of his scalp, and the rest of his hair was jet black. The effect was unmistakably skunk-like. And as for the doctor, all the charm that Bronwyn had witnessed upon their first meeting had evaporated. The couple seemed down and, in fact, quite frail. She didn't understand it, and she didn't feel comfortable asking.

Thankfully, Royce walked into the library carrying baby Serena, and Dr. Kupolou's face lit up.

"May I?" she said, stretching her arms out for Serena. Royce gleefully passed Dr. Kupolou the baby.

Suddenly, the doorbell rang. The butler excused himself to answer it. Bronwyn forced an anxious smile. "They're here."

She pulled Royce over to her side and held his hand. Her palm was sweaty.

The butler re-entered the library, announcing the guests, as if they were all in a scene from *Downton Abbey*.

"Queen Karen of California, and her two sons, Prince Bryce and Prince Kyle."

The queen strode through the double doors looking absolutely nothing like what Bronwyn had expected—she certainly didn't look like any sort of royalty Bronwyn was familiar with.

The woman was tall, like her sons—very tall, practically NBA height. But everything else about the queen's style was full-on Stevie Nicks. She wore a bright green kimono with a raspberry-colored fringe peppering the edges. Tucked into her layered skirt was a ruffly blouse that made her look like a pirate wench. The only thing vaguely royal about her was a strange headpiece she wore that looked like a modified turquoise squash blossom necklace.

"Howdy, hey there!" Queen Karen beamed, galloping her way over to her hosts. "Royce and Bronwyn Langley! I am so excited to meet you both! OTN is just about the only thing I watch. You two—"

She wagged her finger at them and continued her fawning.

"You two *geniuses* are the only ones who have it all figured out! What's going on with this election, huh? My lands! If we have to endure four years of another *libtard*, then I might just have to pack up the colony and move to the coast of Texas with Elon Musk!"

She leaned over, intruding on Bronwyn's personal space and

whispered, "That girlfriend of his? The one that had his baby... *she's* one of us. She's told everyone she is from Canada. Not true! California, deep water, baby!"

The princes saddled appreciatively up to the bar, sneaking in a quick shot of tequila before their mother noticed.

"Boys!"

They scurried over.

"Don't be rude. Introduce yourselves."

"I'm Prince Bryce," one said.

"Prince Kyle," said the other.

They were all long arms and legs... indistinguishable, really. Their mother waved them away.

"Just call them Thing One and Thing Two. That's what I do." Then the queen paused for a moment before going in for a group hug with Royce and Bronwyn. "I really am so honored to be here!"

Bronwyn, spine rigid, plastered on a smile and backed away as politely as possible. The truth was that as much vitriol as OTN peddled, Bronwyn had a high level of disdain for the network's *true fans* like Queen Karen. They creeped her out.

Royce, however, connected with the audience in a much more hearty and authentic way.

"Well, will you look at this," he puffed up proudly, "this is the very first queen I've ever hosted in my house, and she's a salt-of-the-earth, kind-hearted conservative. You honestly cannot get much better than that!" He took both of her hands in his, and they wiggled together, like they were doing some kind of secret handshake that began with a fish dance.

"Champagne?" Bronwyn asked the queen, trying to change the subject.

Queen Karen wrinkled her nose. "Don't really love the stuff."

"Oh, all right," Bronwyn teetered a little. "Something else?"

"A margarita would be amazing, Bronwyn. No salt, and a double shot of the hard stuff."

* * *

Bronwyn found dinner miserable. Not only did Queen Karen have the nerve to reject the specially-prepared vegan meal, she had asked for steak as a replacement. The chefs whipped up well-done meat and fluffy potatoes as quickly as they could. The woman even wanted ketchup with it.

Typical, Bronwyn sneered privately.

After hours of small talk, and Royce chattering away about the state of American politics, Queen Karen finally sat back in her chair, sipping on yet another margarita.

"Thing One," Queen Karen didn't look up as she addressed her son, "let's give the Langleys a play-by-play from the mermaids on our side of the field."

Kyle opened his mouth to speak, but before he could talk, Queen Karen dismissed him. "Not you. No, no... the other one."

"But I'm Thing One," Kyle explained.

She scrunched her face at him, as if trying to discern his features. "Are you? Fine, go on."

"I'm not at liberty to discuss confidential Pan-Atargatic strategy, Mother."

"Nonsense, I don't know why we still have that council. It's as useless as the U.N. Anyway, isn't it all blown up now, after everything Queen Awa's done?"

"Ostensibly, yes, but—"

Queen Karen cut him off again. "See, this is why I don't have time for politicking." She turned to Royce, "Too much blah blah, do you know what I mean?"

Royce bobbed his head in agreement.

"Let's cut to the chase." The queen shifted her eyes toward Dr. Kupolou. "Look, I know Queen Zale executed your little girls. And I am very sorry about that."

Bronwyn's heart jumped.

Someone executed their little girls? No wonder Dr. Kupolou and her husband have been so withdrawn.

She knew precisely the kind of grief the couple must be shouldering. And yet, the doctor had still treated Serena with the kindest, lightest touch. Bronwyn found a new admiration for the doctor's strength and restraint.

Dr. Kupolou's husband stared at his plate, silent as the grave.

Queen Karen began speaking to the couple in Atargatis. "Queen Zale has sent word to me of your betrayal." Her voice was deeper and much more menacing than when she spoke English. "Your Queen wants it to be known that there is but one path for you to return home. She requires that you be an instrument of her will in the world of Man. Do you see how easily Man is led astray by cunning words and flattery? For now, you will say and do everything that your human hosts ask of you. Is that understood?"

"Yes, Queen Karen," Dr. Kupolou replied in Atargatis. She nudged her husband.

"Understood," he whispered, in English.

Queen Karen turned to the Langleys, "Just a little friendly chit-chat in our mother tongue. Here's the bottom line, Royce and Bronwyn, you have united and unwavering support from my colony in California, the Greek colony, and our allies."

The couple offered their thanks, but inside Bronwyn was reeling.

Child murderers, Bronwyn thought, *we're supposed to rely on the help of child murderers? What kind of sick people have we climbed into bed with? Not even Gia would kill a child.*

34

November 1st

"Alone at last," Riley said, closing the door to her apartment. Gia had instructed her security detail to wait in the hallway.

Examining the space, Gia took in the scene. Riley lived in a big glass building situated at the edge of the Hudson River. The ceilings of the apartment soared twenty feet high, and there were no walls, but rather a system of curtains that could be pulled to cordon off spaces, heightening a feeling of intimacy. A grand piano stretched out in the sunken living room.

"Do you play?" Gia asked.

"Sure, of course. I was a musical theater kid. Would you like me to serenade you?"

Gia wrinkled her eyes and forced a smile.

Riley burst out laughing. "Jesus! That is a no if I've ever seen one. Note to self... Gia hates music. What else can I offer you? Hmmm. What about a little kush?"

"Now, *that* I can accept. Gladly."

Riley popped open the freezer and took out a tupperware

container, removing a few tight green buds, which she placed in a grinder. After a moment or so, she had rolled the most exquisite joint.

Gia clapped her hands. "Impressive, *brava*!"

Riley edged closer to Gia, who was leaning on the kitchen island.

"Open your lips," Riley ordered.

Gia spread her lips, and Riley slid the joint into her mouth. She held a lighter out and Gia inhaled. She blew the smoke into Riley's mouth. Riley breathed deeply and held it in her lungs for as long as she could.

"Mmmm," Gia closed her eyes and nodded. "This was a very good idea, Riley."

"You don't know it, but this is all part of my evil plan. First I fill you with illegal drugs, then I get you to tell me all your dirty secrets, and then I fuck you senseless."

"Is that so?"

"Come sit." Riley escorted Gia to an overstuffed couch near the window. She slid the large panels back, and a rush of cold air tickled their skin.

"Lila," Riley said, waking up her virtual assistant, "turn on the fireplace." A thin glass box rose from the floor by the window, and blue flames ignited. Riley stepped away for a moment and returned with a cashmere blanket and two warm rum drinks.

Gia had to admit that she had not felt this cozy in quite some time. No reporters. No pressure. Not even the constant buzzing thought in her mind about how to play the situation and gain the upper hand. Maybe it was the weed, or maybe it was being around Riley, but she felt incredibly relaxed.

Riley lifted the blanket and snuggled up next to Gia, whispering to her, "Can I tell you a secret?"

"What is it?"

Gia watched a wry smirk spread across Riley's face.

"I saw you with Nico once."

Gia snapped out of her comfy daze, but she tried not to telegraph on her face the sense of anxiety hearing Nico's name brought to her chest.

"Relax," Riley cooed, sensing Gia's nerves, "all I wanted to say was that I was sorely jealous of that son of a bitch."

Gia didn't reply, making no comments or gestures.

Riley's eyes lowered to her glass, and she dipped her finger inside it briefly. "I… uh—"

She cleared her throat before continuing.

"I have some fantasies," Riley's voice trembled a little. "They aren't really *normal* fantasies. Ah… I don't know how to say this exactly. And I would never feel comfortable telling anyone else, but I feel like you will understand me."

"Go on."

"Sometimes I touch myself thinking about you killing Nico."

Gia's heart pumped extra blood. She tried to slow her breathing, but was finding herself feeling confused about what to do.

Riley glanced up, hooking into Gia's brown eyes.

"Am I a creep?" Riley asked.

"When you think about that, do you come?"

Riley bit her lip and then smiled. "Very hard."

"Then we better call the doctors immediately and tell them to bring you a straightjacket," Gia replied, turning her eyes toward the fire.

"Ha ha, very funny."

They sat in silence for a while, sipping their drinks.

Riley leaned her head onto Gia's shoulder and angled her mouth toward Gia's ear, breathing into it as she spoke, "My guess is that we're more alike than you even realize."

Then Riley bit Gia's neck so hard that Gia cried out in pain.

35

New Year's Eve 1995

Florent ordered the most expensive bottle of champagne on the menu. He pulled Louisa close to him and buried his head in her long dark hair, imagining, as he had quite often in the past week, that she was Gia. The band played, and the curtains went up at La Perle Noire.

Dimitri danced his way onto the stage, and Louisa sat up.

"The show is starting!" she said eagerly, kissing Florent's cheek. The club had been making quite a splash across Europe since Gia took ownership, and Louisa was thrilled to be in Paris with Florent, celebrating at the nude revue. She felt quite chic and sophisticated.

Florent watched Dimitri's every move, reliving their moments together.

During the second performance, while the audience was focused on a bare-breasted chorus line, Dimitri snuck over to Florent's banquette and slid in.

"Hello, stranger," Dimitri whispered to Florent.

"This is Louisa, *my girlfriend*," Florent replied, flashing Dimitri a look he made sure that Louisa could not see.

Dimitri knew what *that* look meant all too well.

It was the ever-insistent way of conveying "I'm straight," and Florent wasn't the first of Dimitri's closeted lovers to look at him this way.

Tiresome, but Dimitri played along.

Dimitri took Louisa's hand, kissing it, "*Bonsoir,* you magnificent creature. Happy New Year."

"The same to you," she giggled.

Dimitri noticed her accent and spoke to her in Italian, asking her where she was from.

"*Milano,*" she explained to him in her native language, "but I go to school with Florent in Geneva. How do you two know each other?"

"Ah, I was a good friend of his father's."

Florent interrupted the Italian conversation. "If you're talking about me, Dimitri, you better be saying nice things."

"But, of course!" he replied to Florent in French. "I always wait until after the first bottle of champagne is finished before I start gossiping. Anyway, I must run. It has been enchanting to meet you, beautiful Louisa. Florent, I wish you the happiest New Year, and may next year be better than the last." He leaned in to peck Florent on the cheek and then whispered in his ear, "I mean that. I am very sorry, Florent." He waved to Louisa and dashed off.

Florent turned to his girlfriend, "Oh, I forgot to ask him something. I'll be right back." Before she had a chance to respond, he was off, running after Dimitri, whom he caught up to just before disappearing backstage. "Dimitri, wait," he called out. "I… I saw Gia here in Paris on Christmas Eve. I went by the apartment building a few times, but I couldn't find her again."

"Florent," Dimitri sighed, "you need to forget about her."

"I can't."

"She's moved on, Florent. You have that sweet, lovely girl out there. You should focus on her. Gia is beyond your depth."

Beyond my depth? The words stung him.

"I was already deep inside that bitch, Dimitri, so she is in no way *beyond* me."

"Sweet boy, you were deep inside me also, but you can't even be honest about that with your little girlfriend. Grow up."

"Fuck you."

"See what I mean?" Dimitri snapped. "You're just a kid."

"If you speak to Gia," Florent said, turning his back on Dimitri, "tell her that I *will* find her."

36

November 16th

Gia's escalade rolled to a stop in front of 60 Lafayette Street in lower Manhattan. Large san serif letters hung above the entrance: NEW YORK FAMILY COURT.

The building, with its exterior of flat grey stone tiles, was outdated. Apart from the garish lettering announcing its true purpose, the facade looked very little like a courthouse and rather more like a rundown office building.

Gia's makeup artist dabbed a bit of powder on her and reapplied her soft berry-colored lipstick before her security detail opened the doors to the screaming crowd. Beside Gia walked *La Nonna* and a small army of men in red ties and blue suits, partners from the top litigation firm Cohen, Cohen, Lance, and Briar.

Then the Langleys arrived. It was only Royce, Bronwyn, their lawyer Huntington, and one security guard. Traveling lightly must have been a play to make them look more relatable. It was smart. Bronwyn made a point to stop in front of the courthouse and embrace Gia, afterward handing Serena to her to hug and carry inside. The gesture, while purely a photo op meant to portray

Bronwyn as a generous grandmother, caught Gia off guard. She cradled Serena in her arms and smelled her hair. The paparazzi furiously snapped photos.

The security guards were forced to surrender their weapons and check them at a holding station before passing through a metal detector. The line for the elevators was considerable, forcing Gia to endure a long stretch of time standing next to the Langleys.

Gia glared at Bronwyn. "I hope you understand that I will not let you keep my child. It does not matter what I have to do to get her back. She will be coming home to Europe with me."

Instead of answering, Bronwyn simply flashed a disingenuous smile.

Inside the small courtroom, a bailiff showed the parties to their respective tables before beginning the proceedings.

Towering over the room, at the judge's bench, was the Honorable Zenobia Nwadike. Gia observed the woman, trying to glean any discernible information from her body language, but there was nothing unusual. Judge Nwadike had a serious, but not sour look on her face, and her dark hair was braided elegantly into a bun crown.

The bailiff announced the case, "Matter of Acquaviva versus Langley, all rise." They did. Judge Nwadike knocked her gavel, and the case was officially open.

Huntington spoke first. "Your Honor, if it please the court, we would like to move for summary judgment in favor of the Langleys."

"On what grounds?" Judge Nwadike inquired.

"Your Honor, we have here a document, signed by Miss Acquaviva, that grants full custody of baby Serena Francesca to Royce and Bronwyn Langley, her grandparents."

"May I see this, please?" The judge waved Huntington up to the bench.

Before going, he passed a copy to *La Nonna*. She nudged the first chair lawyer, Sid Cohen, and he rose to address the judge.

"Apologies, Your Honor, but we were given no prior notice of either this document nor Mr. Huntington's intent to raise it as cause for dismissing this case."

"Noted, Mr. Cohen," the judge replied. "However, I would like to review the document in question." She took the stapled pages from Huntington and flipped through them. "This seems comprehensive, but this custody agreement has not previously been filed with the proper channels to certify it and properly grant guardianship to the Langleys. Why is that?"

"Your Honor," Huntington said, leaning forward, "the circumstances in this case have been rather extraordinary. You see, at the time that my clients took possession of the child—"

"Stole the child!" Sid shouted, shooting up from the desk and stomping to the bench. "Let's be very clear here. We have filed a Hague Convention violation for the improper removal of this child from her rightful home in Italy. Mere hours after Ms. Acquaviva gave birth, Serena was kidnapped. The babe was ripped from her mother's breast and taken to a foreign country!"

The judge banged her gavel. "Order! Mr. Cohen, lower the tone of your voice. I will not tolerate outbursts in my courtroom."

"Understood. My apologies, Your Honor."

"Mr. Huntington," the judge continued, "is it true that the Langleys removed Serena improperly?"

"Your Honor, at the time that my clients came to Italy, the police were raiding Ms. Acquaviva's house with an arrest warrant for murder. These were extenuating circumstances, and they were acting out of great care and love and in the best interest of their grandchild."

"I see," the judge replied.

La Nonna signaled to Sid to come to the table, and she whispered something in his ear. She then reached into her briefcase and pulled out a paper. Sid then reapproached the bench.

"Your Honor," Sid explained, "This is a document... both the original in Italian, as well as an English translation, that clears Gia Acquaviva from any wrongdoing with the unfortunate and messy police mixup to which Mr. Huntington is alluding."

Huntington cleared his throat. "Regardless, Your Honor, it is my client's belief, and my intent to show the court, that Miss Acquaviva is an unfit mother, and that the best interest of the child is for full custody to be awarded to her grandparents. You see, Miss Acquaviva lives a high-risk lifestyle that would expose her daughter to unlawful activity, put her in proximity to drugs, prostitution, organized crime, and a highly unstable home life."

"Excuse me, Your Honor," Sid fumed, "and sincere apologies for the anger in my voice, but never in my career have I seen an attorney prattle on about unfounded and fantastical claims. In fact, if Mr. Huntington continues in this manner, we will file a suit for defamation of character. Furthermore, Your Honor, it is *our* intention to show you, without question, that the only people unfit to raise this child are Royce and Bronwyn Langley. After all, we are dealing with a first-of-its-kind case here. This is not any ordinary child. Serena Francesca *Acquaviva* is a mermaid. As such, she has special needs, for which only her mother can provide. In fact, recently," he paused to flag down one of his partners, who rushed to the stand with a folder, "the child was taken to an *animal* hospital for treatment, because her grandparents were so unequipped to deal with raising a merbaby, that they nearly poisoned her to death!"

Huntington smiled and winked at Sid. "You know, Mr. Cohen, I am so glad you brought that up, because we have also brought to court an affidavit from the very doctor who treated baby Serena at the hospital. That doctor is now living full-time at the Langley's compound, and is offering the child round-the-clock care. And that doctor, Your Honor, is a mermaid."

"Gentlemen," the judge wove her arms, causing the men to take a few steps back, "while this is all very interesting, you are both well aware that this is not the proper chain of proceedings for a case such as this. Lawyers do not come and scream at the edge of my bench and toss papers and recriminations. There is a process, and we will follow it. I do appreciate that this is a highly unusual case, and that it might cause passions to run high, but I ask that next time we convene, you sit back and let me drive the ship. Now, take your seats."

The men gathered their papers and dashed egos, returning to their respective sides.

"Now," the judge exhaled, "please submit your briefs and all the related documentation for me to review in due time. The first order of business is that I will be requesting a home evaluation at the Langleys to determine if, indeed, that is where this child should be staying during these proceedings, or if temporary custody should be awarded to the child's mother. Please schedule a hearing with the clerk once the home study has been completed."

The judge lowered the gavel again, ending the court session.

37

November 17th

The studio lights were even hotter than *La Nonna* had imagined they would be. She certainly was not in the habit of making public statements for clients, because, up until she began her dealings with Gia, her clients had been the kind of businesspeople who preferred to be known only in a very small circle... preferring to keep any dirty laundry in their families' backyards—and not in a watery graveyard under a Venetian hotel.

Before the camera went live, Harper walked over to *La Nonna* to greet her. "You look nervous," Harper said, eyeing the anxious lines around the old woman's mouth.

"*Madonna!* Look at the size of that camera! In Italy we say that everything is bigger in America. Now I know that these words are true!"

Harper nodded. "I get it. It's very intimidating when you come in for the first time. Just think of the camera as a person. When you look into the lens, imagine that you're gazing into the eyes of your best friend. And once you think about it like that, the camera isn't some weird machine, it's like a person you've known forever."

"If you say so, *piccolina*!"

They took their places, and Harper's crew notified her that it was time to go on air.

"Good evening, LION viewers, and thank you for tuning in. Yet again, our top story is Mermaid Gia Acquaviva. Look, I just have to say this for the record... to be honest, it's not easy to have my family tangled up in this very public and highly controversial story. Between us, I really do wish that my brother Cameron was here, and that he and Gia could visit my parents, just like a normal couple would. It's especially difficult with the holidays coming up. I was with Gia and Cam last Thanksgiving... strangely enough at my parents' house. If I had known back then that it would be my last holiday with my brother, believe me, I would have acted differently. I don't normally talk about my feelings on air, but at this time, I think it's really important that I do that, because this isn't just some news story to me... it's my family. I always do my *absolute best* to remain impartial. I hope you know that." Harper took a deep, cleansing breath. "Now, shifting back to the events of the day... today we are joined by Donatella Sapiente, who is Gia Acquaviva's attorney. If you've been reading the news, her face is probably recognizable to you. Donatella, welcome to the show."

The camera cut to a wide angle, and *La Nonna,* who was perched in the chair at the long desk, folded her arms on the table to attempt to appear as if she belonged there. "*Buonasera*, Harper. Thank you for having me. It is a great joy."

Harper scrunched her eyebrows into a judgey arch, "Okay, sure." She glanced up at the teleprompter for her cue. "So, yesterday was an important day in the custody battle for my niece, The Little Mermaid, Serena. You had your first day in court. How did that go?"

"You tell me, Harper. What did your parents tell you about the hearing?"

Harper scoffed, before easing into a smirk, "We're not exactly on speaking terms these days."

"No?" *La Nonna* probed, voice climbing an octave. "How strange... so you are telling me that your parents are not able to maintain a good relationship with their *own daughter*? That is very interesting indeed. And yet, they present themselves as such capable caretakers in front of the correct authority figures."

"Excuse me! My private interactions with my parents are not fodder, meant to be used against them."

"Oh, but Harper, you see, once a court custody case has begun, private matters become public. You must invite the long arm of the law into your life... and let it... mmm... how do you say... open the curtains in the living room for a while."

"Ha! Really? Then I assume that means Gia is willing to open her curtains as well? You know, in the spirit of truth."

"*Signorina* Acquaviva has been incredibly gracious and open with the media, do you not agree, Harper?"

"Sure, sure... if you think fluff pieces in *Vogue* qualify as investigative journalism! Also, I feel I need to point out that Gia has been asked to come on this program *numerous* times and has thus far refused."

La Nonna beamed, wholly unperturbed by Harper's needling. "Why do you need Gia's beautiful face when you have mine?"

"Mrs. Sapiente—"

"Please, call me *La Nonna*. This is what I am known by in Italy."

"*La Nonna*? Could you please explain to the viewers... and to me... what that means? My Italian is not very good."

"I am a grandmother, and so all my clients call me by that title, which is *La Nonna*. Understand? Ah! *Allora*, this brings me to an important point. As a grandmother myself, I have a lot of empathy for your parents. I love my grandchildren. I have five! Maybe six... but my daughter-in-law is being a bit secretive about a possible new pregnancy..." *La Nonna* smiled at the thought. "Anyway!" she returned to the point at hand. "Believe me when I tell you that I love my grandchildren so much, but I also understand that they belong with their parents. It is very important for a child's development that they live with their biological parents whenever possible. Which is why your niece should be with her mother."

"It's my understanding that yesterday in court my parents alleged that Gia had previously signed over all custody rights to them. Is that true?"

"Impossible."

"What?"

"This agreement that you mention was signed under duress and it is therefore invalid."

Harper shook her head, not comprehending. "Sorry, what do you mean it was *signed under duress*?"

"I cannot reveal more information about that matter at this time." *La Nonna* tilted her head casually toward her interviewer. "Harper, have you considered having children?"

Harper pressed her lips together, clearly annoyed and refusing to be sidetracked. "No deflecting, please. Are you saying my parents *forced* Gia to sign a custody agreement?"

"In a manner of speaking."

"That doesn't make any sense."

"Oh, but it makes perfect sense, Harper, and one day soon you will understand just how truly evil your parents really are."

Harper whipped toward the camera and spoke to the viewers. "This is too much to process on air. These allegations are immense and possibly have far-reaching consequences." She angled toward *La Nonna* again, "Before we continue this line of discussion on air, I'm going to need to see some physical evidence."

La Nonna nodded. "It would be my great pleasure to show you."

38

November 20th

The room smelled of sex and spilled cocktails. In the performance circle at Gia's Berlin club, porn star Buck Angel was stripped down to a white tank top and nothing else. His tattooed body was lifted into the air and settled into a rope swing by a group of eager submissives. From there, a Shibari master wove elegant knots around Buck's torso until he was immobilized. Buck was then elevated ever so slightly off the ground. The domme spread Buck's legs, and let the submissives take turns licking Buck's clit.

Moussa observed the action from a corner. No doubt, it was a beautiful show—decadent and sensual—but without Oumar by his side, life had become a palette of greys. At times, he felt like he was trapped inside a Kerry James Marshall painting, never able to escape the confines of his dark canvas, his mind forever oiled by grief. He often found himself wondering, *Is this it? What's the point of it all?*

So lost was he in his melancholy that he failed to notice a pair of blonde heads wading through the crowd—their eyes trained directly on Moussa.

"Moussa!" Kyle shouted over the loud music, going in for a hug.

Moussa backed up on instinct, "Why are *you two* here?" He glanced from one brother to the next, narrowing his eyes suspiciously.

"Is that any way to greet an old friend?" Bryce chided.

"Friend? You cannot be serious," snorted Moussa derisively.

Bryce shrugged.

"Look—"

Before Bryce could finish his thought, Moussa cut him off, speaking to the men in a baby voice, "Did your *maman* send you here, wittle boys? Queen Karen mad! Queen Karen make big, bad temper tantrum!"

"Wow," Bryce scoffed, closing the space between himself and Moussa, "that's rich for a kid who can't even get his startup off the ground without his own mommy running around half of Asia, chasing financing for him."

"Guys, enough," Kyle said, stepping between them before things got any more heated. "Our mother doesn't know we're here. We came because we care about you, and we care about the relationship between our two nations. If Queen Awa continues on this path with the public threats and disclosing confidential information that has been secret for centuries, then there will be severe consequences."

"Do you really *think* she doesn't know that?" Moussa replied. "As if she has not taken that into account before she took action?"

"Moussa," Kyle's voice was shaky, and its timbre set Moussa's hair on end, "this is deadly serious. People will die. It's one thing to play a little tit for tat on land, but what these two queens are cooking up... it's fucked."

"*Chéri*," Moussa reached out and laid his hand on Kyle's, "I appreciate this information, I do. But the ship has set sail. As much as it pains me to be *at odds* with *old friends*, I stand firmly beside my mother... not behind her, mind you. And whatever comes, so be it. May the Gracious Tides be with me."

Bryce and Kyle shook their heads in disbelief and disappointment, turning to go. But then Kyle whipped around and pointed an angry finger at Moussa.

"Get the fuck back to Senegal, Moussa, and batten down the hatches. A fucking tidal wave is about to shake up your shit and change things *forever*."

39

January 1996

Florent placed Louisa's hand luggage on the floor as they looked up at the airport monitor to see if their flight to Geneva had been assigned a gate.

As he scanned the cities, he thought of Gia. *Berlin... could she be there? Monte Carlo perhaps? Maybe she is back in Venice.*

To Louisa, it felt as if he was a million miles away. "Is everything all right, Florent?"

He ignored her. He'd been ignoring her all day.

In fact, he'd been distant and cold since New Year's Eve. She couldn't imagine how difficult it must have been to be without his father. She was extremely close to both of her parents, so she extended him the grace and understanding that she would have wanted had she been suffering through something equally as painful.

For his part, Florent had been totally absorbed in a silent search for Gia. Every place he took Louisa was part of his hunting effort. He ran mental facial recognition on every person in the crowd. He racked his brain trying to imagine where she was and who she was with. He only wished he'd paid more attention to the man he had seen her with, because that man might hold a clue.

"I am going to buy a magazine," Louisa said.

He nodded and she walked off as he collapsed into a chair and tried to calm his mind. Louisa returned a few moments later with her magazine and two coffees.

"*Paris Match*, really, Louisa?" he chided.

"Oh, be quiet. I enjoy reading the tabloids while I am traveling. Anyway, soon I will have my head in a book, so let me have my fun."

"Entertain me," he laughed. "Read me some of these very important, newsworthy stories."

She read aloud as he glanced down at the pages. There were long form interviews with celebrities and Euro royals, but Louisa's favorite sections were the pages with paparazzi photos.

It was then that something shocking caught Florent's eye. There was a photo of a famous French singer exiting a restaurant. Just behind the door of the restaurant was a woman whose face was partially obscured, but Florent would have recognized her anywhere: It was Gia.

40

Thanksgiving Day

Talia ferried Gia from her apartment at Excalibur to 77th and Central Park West at the ass crack of dawn. The parade marshals were already lining up the various groups, readying them for deployment along the West side of Central Park, past Columbus Circle, and finally to the parade's end at Herald Square.

The sky was thick with enormous balloons... Snoopy, Mickey, a gigantic gobbling turkey... all powered by the feet of an army of wranglers.

Gia wondered if one person continued to hold onto the big balloon while everyone else let go at the same time, would that unfortunate soul simply float away into the clouds?

ADET had taken some of their big donor money and invested in three mobile LED billboards. Gia's job was to sit at the helm of that gaudy armada. ADET's official partnership with Gia would be announced that day, live on television. Perfect timing, really. Talia and Lee had cooked up the idea so that ADET could receive maximum press coverage, not only to increase awareness of their organization and Gia's custody case, but also to take advantage of millions of eyeballs and promote veganism.

The horde of ADET activists present for the parade had been given strict instructions *not* to pull any stunts like throwing red paint on fur. Rather, they were to focus on passing out flyers with Tofurkey recipes and pamphlets explaining the horrific conditions in which turkeys were kept prior to their slaughter.

As the parade kicked off, Gia graced the throne that sat atop the first billboard truck, and Lee signaled to the driver to cue up the lights. The huge television screens played a looped video, shot by David LaChapelle, of Gia swimming underwater, her pearlescent tail sparkling against the bright blue of the water. In a clever trick, the image had been split across the three trucks, so that Gia seemed to swim seamlessly between the screens. The size of the billboards made her appear nearly thirty times larger than she was in real life.

Just as expected, when the mermaid caravan rolled south through Manhattan, the parade watchers went wild. A few times, the crowd broke into a spontaneous up and down wave, like at a baseball game, making the sidewalk mimic a rocking ocean made of people.

Gia heard her name screamed thousands and thousands of times. The sensation of all that adoration was strange and somehow isolating. Even though she was surrounded by security, she knew she was still totally exposed, and she imagined that this was what daily life must feel like for popes, presidents, and pop stars.

As she waved at the crowd with a forced beatific gaze, her thoughts drifted to Nico. He had always begged her to come with him to public events, and she rejected his pleas every time.

He wanted me as a shield. Now I understand why.

In a way, this was a fitting punishment for Gia. Being the object of global fascination placed her in Nico's shoes. She had no choice but to empathize with him... insofar as she was actually able to feel anything at all.

Gia then pictured herself trapped in Q's aquarium, and for the first time realized that may not have been the prison she had considered it to be. She would never have had to experience the crushing weight of fame.

Is this really freedom?

At the press point in Columbus Circle, the ADET trucks made a planned stop. Gia's security team helped her down for an interview with the cable news channel covering the parade.

Gia was joined by ADET's CEO, Alicia Alvarez, a Cuban-American long-time philanthropic leader, and a fixture in the NGO ecosystem. Alicia was extremely savvy and adept at steering absolutely any conversation with the media back to her talking points. While Alicia had at first been skeptical of the partnership with Gia, Lee had convinced Alicia that this would be a huge step in taking ADET mainstream. After witnessing how the crowd reacted to seeing Gia live and in person, Alicia knew that their bet had paid off handsomely. Without the halo of mystique that surrounded Gia, never in a million years would morning television have given ADET the opportunity to spread a message about the ethical treatment of animals.

All around Columbus Circle the echo of the crowd was so loud that Gia and Alicia were given earplugs, and rather than answering questions live, since they could not hear a good goddamn thing, they instead read captions of what the anchor was saying, so they could respond.

The conversation ping-ponged back and forth without any gotcha moments. It was as friendly of an interview as Gia had had thus far in her public life. The reporter even gave Alicia a solid sixty seconds for ADET promotion. You could not pay advertising dollars for this kind of exposure.

As the crowd chanted "GIA, GIA, GIA!" it was hard for her to ignore a gnawing sense of dread at her core.

What will happen to me if all of this love turns to hate?

* * *

In the late afternoon, ADET hosted a vegan feast at the Rainbow Room at Rockefeller Center. Gia glittered at the head table. She wore a creamy strapless gown with a crystal-encrusted cape draped over both shoulders.

When a quiet moment presented itself, she took a moment to skulk over to the twenty-foot-tall windows and take in the view. Directly across from her was the crown of the Empire State Building. It seemed as though she could wrap her arms around it, like a steel sequoia tree.

Here she was, floating at the top of Manhattan in the most iconic ballroom, staring at the city's most exemplary view, and yet, she felt utterly alone.

Gia lifted a glass of champagne from a silver tray and sighed before taking a sip. She closed her eyes for a moment and let herself imagine Cameron strolling up behind her, smiling ear to ear, and then brushing her hair to the side, just before kissing the nape of her neck.

"Hello, beautiful." Gia felt a warm breath against her earlobe, and for a moment, she allowed herself to pretend that it was Cam.

Of course it was not.

The whisper belonged to Riley Rose.

Riley took Gia by the hand. "Come with me," she said.

As they turned, the room parted, all eyes on the couple as they escaped for a moment alone.

There was no doubt about it; they looked good together. Riley slipped behind a curtain and Gia followed. They pushed through an emergency exit door and into a dim stairwell.

"Jesus, Gia," Riley eyed her up and down, "you're giving me a hard-on right now."

Riley pressed Gia against the wall and kissed her. She threaded the long fingers of her left hand into Gia's hair and tugged. Her other hand traced Gia's body from her waist, up past her breasts, to her neck. Riley raised her forearm and pressed it under Gia's chin, choking her lightly. "You're so fucking beautiful that you make me want to break your bones."

Gia found herself taken in by the violence in Riley's words. She arched her body, closing the space between herself and Riley.

"Do you like this, Gia?" Riley's eyes sunk their little hooks into Gia's. The latter answered the question with an enthusiastic kiss. Riley then gathered Gia's skirt and explored everything below it.

Gia's cape fell off her shoulders, crashing onto the concrete steps in a shatter, as crystals flew everywhere. Riley and Gia moved together to the top of the stairs, where Riley splayed Gia's legs, tracing the elastic edges of Gia's soaked panties. She bit Gia's thigh as she slid two fingers inside, and then three. When Gia moved her hips in time with Riley's hands, Riley pulled her closer. "I'm going to put everything inside you now, okay?"

"Everything?" Gia asked, confused.

"My fist."

Gia nodded, and Riley made a spear with her fingers, pushing very, very slowly inside of Gia. At the knuckles, Riley helped things along by licking Gia's clit. Everything was juicy. When Riley's hand was inside Gia practically to the wrist, Riley simply let Gia move in the way that pleased her.

"Gia, close your eyes," Riley commanded. "Think about slitting my throat while I'm still inside you like this. Imagine my hot blood trickling down your naked body."

Gia felt her orgasm cascading from some deeper place inside of herself. It vibrated slowly at first. Riley took hold of Gia's cheek with her free hand and said, "I'm going to slap you now, you dirty little slut."

As Riley's hand struck Gia's face, the pain spread and met with the intense contractions between her legs.

Gia came so hard that she screamed.

41

December 1st

The social worker scrutinized the unmarked vial, holding it up to her eye, then unscrewing the top and smelling the liquid inside.

"So what is this, exactly?" she asked Bronwyn.

"It's a hormone that keeps Serena's legs in place."

"You're giving this baby a *hormone*?" The social worker's eyes grew wide as she scribbled notes in a folder that she held close to her body.

"It's perfectly safe," Bronwyn insisted.

"I see. And why is it that you don't want her tail to be in its natural state?"

Bronwyn balked, "It's not that we don't *want* her to show her tail... it's just easier to... manage things when she has her legs. Right honey?" she said, kicking Royce's ankle under the table.

He glanced up from his cell phone, where he had been furiously responding to emails. "What?"

"Darling," Bronwyn tried to keep her voice level, "this nice woman Rebecca—"

"My name is Rachel," the social worker interrupted.

Bronwyn grimaced. "Oh my, I'm so sorry. Royce, *Rachel* was asking why Serena's legs are legs right now."

"*What*?!" he raised his voice, clearly annoyed and confused by the question. In fact, he was exasperated by this whole process. He had a distaste for regulators and bureaucrats that bordered on outright scorn.

"Mr. Langley, administering a *hormone* to keep a *baby mermaid* in her human form because she is more *manageable* seems extreme." Rachel jotted down more notes on her papers.

"Get the doctor down here, then," Royce snapped. "She'll tell you."

"The doctor?" Rachel asked.

Royce focused his eyes back on his phone and mumbled, "The mermaid doctor."

"Why is there a doctor here, Mrs. Langley?"

"Excuse me, Rachel, but is it a crime to give proper care to my grandchild? We moved the doctor in for round-the-clock help."

"Are you saying," Rachel checked a box on a form Bronwyn desperately wanted to get a look at, "that you don't feel confident raising this child on your own without the help of a *live-in doctor*?"

Bronwyn felt her pulse rise and her face flush. "Don't misunderstand me, now. I have raised two children of my own, so I'm more than capable of caring for Serena."

"Two human children?" Rachel asked.

"Do you think we're collecting magical creatures here?" Bronwyn snapped. "Of course they were human!"

"It says here that your son, the father of the child, is deceased."

"He is..." Bronwyn couldn't bring herself to say more, and she pinched herself under the table to keep herself from crying.

"Does Serena have access to other mermaids, or mermaid culture in general?"

"Again, we have a doctor living here who, herself, is a mermaid. Her husband, too."

"Sorry, the doctor's husband lives here also? I'll need to see their accomodations and speak with them. Returning to the question... apart from the child's mother and this *couple* you have living here with you, who in the mermaid community does your grandchild see? Relatives? Perhaps the mermaid grandparents? Friends of the mother?"

"What exactly are you getting at?" Bronwyn's anger was rising, and she could no longer keep it at bay. "My entire goal in life right now is to keep my granddaughter healthy, and to save her from the malicious nature and nefarious activities of her mother. That woman is an unfit mother!"

"You view yourself as a *savior* of the baby?"

"That's not what I said!"

"Actually, Mrs. Langley, that is *exactly* what you implied."

* * *

BRONWYN LOCKED herself in her closet with Serena, sobbing. The rest of the day had not gone as planned, and her grip on the custody situation appeared to be slipping. "Don't worry, little one. Grandma Brownie will keep you safe. I will, baby."

Serena began crying as well, and Bronwyn held her tightly, rocking her, as they sat on the floor together.

Royce rapped at the door, "Darling, come out. You've been in here for hours."

"Go away!" she shrieked. "You screwed up, Royce! I asked you to be mentally present, to help me answer all the questions... and you couldn't put down your phone for five goddamn minutes. You left me to fend for myself with that horrible troll. So just leave me alone!"

He stomped off, unwilling to coax his wife out of what he saw as an overblown tantrum.

Bronwyn's mind fluttered with worries and counter strategies. There was only one card left to play, and it was a risky one. If played correctly, the world would know with certainty who Gia really was.

Bronwyn reached for her phone and dialed Ashley Mason, who answered right away.

"Ashley, I need you to go on air with a new story tonight. Gia murdered Quintilio Mosca, and I have evidence to prove it."

42

December 3rd

"We're in crisis mode here, Gia," Talia insisted. "I need you to trust me."

"I do not understand why I should go on Harper's show. It does not make any sense to me. How can she be seen as impartial?"

"Impartial?! Jesus, the last thing we want is someone to be impartial. We need a voice on our side!"

"And you think *Harper* is that voice?" Gia replied.

"Do you want custody of your child?"

"What kind of question is this? Why would I be here doing all of this otherwise?!"

"Then trust me! Harper is totally disgusted and furious with her parents. She knew nothing about what happened with Quintilio Mosca."

"I cannot trust Harper. She cares only for her own interests."

"And your interests are aligned! She's on the cusp of getting her own cable news show. If you go tonight and do this interview, that will push Goldie over the edge, and then he's going to give Harper what she has always dreamed of.... basically since birth... which is a spot on daytime! Mkay? So, let's go. Suit the fuck up, and let's go slay these beasts. Your alternative is to sit here and be branded a killer *for real*. Like in a provable way."

Gia cursed in Italian before relenting. "Fine. Call in that man who does my hair. I will go."

* * *

THE LAST THING Gia expected was to feel shaken by seeing Harper.

Harper was equally as shaken by the sight of Gia. Harper held cold spoons on her swollen eyes. Her stomach churned. There would be no coming back from betraying her parents publicly like this, and the fallout could be nuclear. But there was too much at stake for her.

Besides, Harper knew of some of her father's misdoings—his friendships with crooked politicians and criminals of all ilk. She always had the feeling that her mother was complicit, but never had any proof. Now she realized the truth: Not only was Bronwyn involved, but she was clearly the mastermind in many of her parents' operations.

The producer talked Gia through the next steps and escorted her to her spot on the set. Harper took her place, and then the familiar studio lights shone on them both.

When the theme music quieted, Harper swallowed and then stared down the lens of the camera.

"Good evening. As you know, I was not on air yesterday. The story that broke on OTN was shocking. We all saw the surveillance tape of Gia attacking and killing Quintilio Mosca. And there is a reason why I did not host my show last night, and it's deeply personal. Today, I will share that story. I am joined by Gia Acquaviva, the mother of my niece, the world's most famous mermaid. We have a truly harrowing revelation to share that will, without a doubt, change the course of my life and the life of my parents."

The camera switched to a wide angle. "Welcome to the show, Gia."

Gia exhaled deeply. "I cannot say that I am glad to be here, Harper."

"Same," Harper snapped back. "Obviously this is very difficult for both of us, so let's not waste time with chit-chat. What are you here to say?"

The jib holding Gia's camera swung around and zoomed in slowly on her face.

"The things that Quintilio Mosca... Q... the things he did to me were—"

Gia's voice broke.

It took a moment before she could regain her composure. She started over, "Ah... he held me against my will. He threatened me with violence daily. Not empty threats, you understand. He killed your brother, Cameron... the love of my life, the father of my child... and Q *loved* that. He talked about having Cameron murdered all the time. Q loved to torture people. Before he held me captive, he sliced up his previous lover, carving pieces off of her until she died. He wanted to keep me locked up for the rest of my life—in an aquarium, no less. He stole from me... more than one hundred million Euros. I cannot express the evil—"

"And that's why you killed him," Harper replied.

"Yes."

"Wow," Harper's eyes widened. "I have to be honest, I didn't expect you to admit that."

"You see, I knew he would hunt me until he had the chance to take me again. So, when your parents gave me the chance to kill him, I had to take it."

"My parents... Royce and Bronwyn Langley. How were they involved?"

"At your brother's funeral they took me to your mother's office and told me that they had abducted Q... and then they said if I would sign a paper to give them custody of Serena, they would let me kill Q."

"They said that?"

"They said that, yes."

"My mother or my father?"

"They both pressured me. They took advantage of me. I still had broken bones and nightmares... and when I was at my most vulnerable point, grieving the loss of your brother, they preyed on me."

"I'm not sorry you killed, Q," Harper admitted. "Given the chance, I might have done it myself. What I am sorry about is that my parents manipulated you and put you in that position so that they could steal your child away from you. It's sick."

Gia lowered her head into her hands.

Then Harper said aloud what she had been thinking since the day before, when Talia and *La Nonna* had called to tell her the whole story.

"My parents are accessories to murder."

43

December 6th

Gia's legal team acted swiftly, requesting an emergency hearing to try to wrestle custody from the Langleys in the wake of this scandal. Obviously, they knew this move would fail. No sane judge would have given Gia custody at this juncture. But it was a long-term play.

First, cast a cloud of doubt over the grandparents, then clear Gia of any possible charges that might arise from the death of Q. Only then would the work begin to cash in on the goodwill of the public to pressure the court into granting Gia custody. All in all, it was a complicated legal strategy, but *La Nonna* felt very good about the odds.

The welfare report and home study were not complete, but nonetheless, Judge Nwadike called the social worker, Rachel, to appear in court that day.

"Your Honor," Huntington said, approaching the bench, "this is a highly unusual course of action to take in this case. I would like to raise an objection to the testimony."

"Mr. Huntington," the judge replied, "your objections can be raised only during cross-examination. You've been in here enough to know that. Now, have a seat and let me get to the bottom of this whole mess."

Huntington shuffled back to his side of the courtroom with the Langleys.

"In all my years on the bench," Judge Nwadike began, "never have I seen something like this. I'm not going to speak to the alleged crimes committed by the parties here today… that's for my friends in the criminal system to sort out. Miss Benson," the judge turned her head to the social worker, "tell me what you observed when you went to the Langleys' house."

Rachel opened her folder to review her notes. "The Langleys have engaged a non-licensed OBGYN to stay in their home. This doctor is preparing home remedies and administering totally unregulated, non-FDA-approved hormones to the baby. The child has not had regular contact with her mother, nor has she had contact with family or family friends of her own species. Mr. and Mrs. Langley have essentially sequestered the child in their home and cut her off from all other influence. In my opinion, the degree of control that they are exerting borders on abusive."

"Objection," Huntington rose from his chair, "the expert has not supplied the data on which she is forming her opinion."

"Mr. Huntington," the judge sneered, "you will be allowed to question Miss Benson during cross-examination and raise your objections then. Rule 4515 allows Miss Benson to state her expert opinion without data and supporting criteria."

"Your Honor," Sid Cohen, Gia's attorney, said as he raised his hand, "if I may, I have a few questions."

"Go on," Judge Nwadike acquiesced.

"Miss Benson, did you observe troubling behavior during your visit to the Langleys?"

"Yes."

"Can you describe this behavior?"

"Mrs. Langley appears to be fixated on the child—borderline obsessed, while Mr. Langley seems to be completely disengaged…

frankly, *disinterested* is probably a better word... in the child or the child's wellbeing."

"You mentioned that the child has little exposure to the outside world?"

"No, sir... not little exposure... no exposure *at all*. She is not allowed to leave the gates. No one is allowed to see her."

"And regarding interaction with her species, could you elaborate, please?"

"The OBGYN is a mermaid, as is her husband, who, strangely enough, lives in the house as well. However, their contact with the child is severely limited. The child has no opportunity to mingle in a mermaid 'pod', as is customary for their species. In fact, the hormones I mentioned earlier are given to the child in an effort to stave off her natural physical state... that is, having a tail... in favor of legs. This does not appear to be for the health of the child, but rather for the comfort level of her grandparents. Mr. Langley seems... well, disgusted... *disgusted* that the child isn't human."

Bronwyn, who was clearly agitated, began whispering to Huntington in a nearly audible way.

"Thank you. No further questions." Sid plopped into his chair beside Gia, thoroughly satisfied.

Huntington approached the social worker. "Miss Benson, how many years have you been working in the family court system?"

"Around ten."

"And in that time how many cases have you handled with merbabies?"

Rachel laughed at the ludicrous question. "Obviously, this is my first."

"I see," Huntington took a moment to scribble onto a legal pad before continuing. "How many research studies have been completed on merbabies or merchildren in general?"

Rachel glared at Huntington before turning her head to the judge. "Do I really have to answer that?"

Judge Nwadike nodded.

"Okay," Rachel said, "the answer is none. No studies have been completed on merchildren. I am applying my very broad knowledge to this specific case."

"Do you think your knowledge applies here?" Huntington tapped his Montblanc pen on the table repeatedly, creating constant clicks like a metronome.

The noise appeared to agitate Rachel. She stared down at his pen when she answered his question, "I don't see why it wouldn't."

Huntington nodded, as if working out an important detail in his mind. "So there is absolutely no research, there are no prior cases, and there are no other known merchildren... and yet, you... in your *expert* opinion, claim to know what's best for Serena? Forgive me, but your assertions strain credulity." He turned to face the judge, eyeing her assertively. "Your Honor, I hope you agree that there is no data and no supporting criteria to back this so-called expert opinion. Personal opinions, gut beliefs, or quote-unquote feelings don't cut it in the court of law."

"Understood," Judge Nwadike acknowledged. "We're not going to solve the question at hand today. However, given the extreme volatility of the circumstances and possible pending murder charges, I am ordering the child be immediately removed from the Langleys' home and placed into the custody of Child Protective Services."

As Judge Nwadike struck her gavel, Bronwyn erupted into tears. Gia's stomach dropped. Her tiny child would now be placed in the hands of total strangers.

44

February 1996

The blue wind whizzed between the trees, over mountains, and across Florent's face as he sliced through the powder on the slopes of St. Moritz. He felt dizzyingly alive.

Louisa wasn't one for the bunny hills either. She'd started skiing at age four with her parents in the Dolomites, but had switched to snowboarding as its popularity grew in the early 90s. She could best Florent if she wanted to—but she knew he had a temper, was highly competitive, and didn't like being shown up. Instead, she skated close to the ground and allowed her body to feel the curves of the earth.

After a few hours of adrenaline, the pair had truly earned a stiff cocktail. They circled up with their friends for après-ski outside a swanky hotel.

Florent peeled off his gloves and picked up his glass, slowly sipping his Hot Toddy. Louisa was thrilled with how kind and attentive he was being to her and to their friends. He'd even paid for the whole trip himself, setting the group up in a cozy chalet.

But it was all a ruse. The real reason for this getaway was, of course, Gia.

Since he'd spotted Gia in Louisa's magazine just after the new year, he'd been doing a deep dive into the background of her new lover, Serge Dupont. Florent often posted to—and frequently monitored—Serge Dupont message boards and chat rooms on AOL and ICQ. A Serge fan had mentioned that the singer always took a week-long vacation at his ski chalet after a big concert. In turn, and with a little more digging, Florent had discovered that the house was located in St. Moritz.

Amazing what you can find on the Internet, Florent mused.

Florent had timed his visit to St. Moritz carefully. He imagined that Gia would avoid Serge's concerts. Concerts would most certainly have cameras, and Gia hated those. She didn't like the spotlight, a fact that Florent was well aware of. He theorized that Gia would travel to St. Moritz a few days after Serge arrived, and that she would likely book the largest suite at the best hotel in case she wanted privacy.

All I have to do is wait for her. She'll come.

And he was right.

The moment he finally spotted Gia seemed to play out in slo-mo for him—and it felt as if every nerve ending in his body stood at attention.

The sun was setting, casting an orange glow onto the snow. It was a perfect moment that he knew would be etched into his memory forever.

She appeared from a wooded path like some kind of rare creature, wearing a white hat and a matching white fur coat. Her dark hair spilled around her shoulders.

His stomach flopped.

He wished for binoculars, so that he could see her up close.

Florent stalked his prey until she disappeared around the building, no doubt entering the lobby of the hotel.

"Are you all right, Florent?" Louisa asked. "You are suddenly quite flushed, *amore*."

Florent never even looked at his girlfriend. Trance-like, he just muttered, "I think I'll go and splash some water on my face," before wandering inside.

He picked up his speed once he was in the hotel. He jetted toward the lobby and entered the cavernous room just as he spied Gia turn down a hallway, toward the elevator. Not missing a beat, he followed her. He watched the elevator doors part, and when she stepped in, so did he.

Finally, he was face to face with Gia. Her eyes locked with his.

He could barely catch his breath—he was so nervous and stirred up. But he managed to speak, summoning a commanding tone.

"You are a difficult woman to find."

45

December 7th

"Harper, I'm very sorry to hear about your niece." Goldie rolled his wheelchair from the window of his office around to the side of his desk.

"Thank you, Goldie," Harper replied, wondering why he'd called her in.

"So what's your plan now?"

"My plan for what? The coverage?"

"The coverage? Good God, I'm not a monster! I do think about things outside of this network, you know. Harper, your family is falling apart right now. I have a very long history with your mother. Almost married her. I probably *should* have married her. Incredible woman. She's got to be devastated right now. Surely it's better for you to take custody of your niece than have that baby flopping around in the system?"

Harper's mouth dropped open at the suggestion. She had never even considered the thought.

"I can't take care of a baby!" she sputtered. "This isn't some 80s movie. I don't know the first thing about children. *I don't even like them.*" She shivered involuntarily.

"Oh, for fuck's sake... who does? That's not the point. That little mermaid is your family."

"Are you *serious* right now, Goldie? Now you're worried about my family? *Now*?"

"Look, I won't deny that if you take custody of the baby that it will be good for our ratings... and for our narrative arc in general. I can be a kind of Daddy Warbucks, while Royce is tied up in legal drama."

Harper stared blankly at Goldie. "I don't know what you want me to say."

"I've taken the liberty of setting up a press conference this evening."

"A *press conference*? For fucking what?"

"I want you to announce that you're going to seek custody of your niece."

But Harper shook her head immediately. "No. I don't want to do that. Why would I do that?"

"Because if you do, Harper, I'm going to give you a daytime show. Not morning, not that lunch-break crap. I'll give you the four o'clock slot."

Harper found herself momentarily at a loss for words, and then the reality of what Goldie was offering hit her.

"Four o'clock? But that's... that's Opal Windspray's spot."

"I'm moving Opal to three."

"Moving Opal to three o'clock? Wait... so you're saying that Opal will *lead into my show*?"

Goldie smirked, a special kind of mischief dancing in his eyes. "And for the first year, she'll be contracted to say, 'Stay tuned for the most exciting new talk show on daytime, *Hello, Harper!*' You'd like that right?"

"*Hello, Harper*?" Her breath quickened, as did her pulse.

"It has a nice ring to it... no telephone pun intended."

Harper felt her happy soul separate from her body and float away.

But almost as fast as she was shot into orbit, she brought herself back down to earth. "Opal would never agree to that."

"Wrong. She already has."

Something exploded in Harper's chest. *This is it. This is the moment. I've done it. Daytime? I'll be huge.*

"So?" Goldie asked. "Will you do it?" He was perched at the edge of his seat, clearly just as thrilled with himself as Harper was with herself.

* * *

THE SCENE WAS DIFFERENT DOWNTOWN. Gia rested her head on Riley's pillow, trying to squeeze out some tears, but her soul was dry.

"How do you feel?" Riley asked, from the neighboring pillow.

"To be honest, Riley, I do not feel much at all."

"That's normal, right?"

"Is it? I have no idea. Sometimes I feel very strong maternal instincts, and then sometimes there is just a black hole where my love should be."

"Sounds like postpartum depression to me."

Gia didn't reply. Talking to Riley felt comfortable... a bit like talking to Vittore sometimes. Except, Vittore would never know her darkest thoughts and her most vile sins. Neither did Riley, but the difference was that Gia knew that Riley could see her for who she really was. After all, Riley hadn't even asked about what happened with Q—hadn't mentioned the tape—didn't seem to care.

Riley looked right past the pretty patina, straight into Gia's raw id.

And Riley liked what she saw.

At least... it appeared to Gia that Riley liked what she saw.

Riley bounced up onto her hands and knees and then crawled on top of Gia, straddling her. "What about this for a plan? First, I go down on you, and then I make us both a really strong cup of coffee?"

"*Una scopata e un caffè?*"

"Mmm, say that again. I don't know what it means, but it sounds so sexy."

"*Una scopata e un caffè.*"

"I love that." Riley kissed Gia's neck and took her time traveling, all the way under the sheets.

46

December 10th

No one stopped Yiannis at the door of the casino in Venice. He breezed in with a crew of Greek cousins like he owned the place—because his intention *was* to own the place.

It was clear to Yiannis that Prince Moussa's people hadn't been trained in security or combat. They were merely eeking by, he observed, barely keeping the roulette wheel spinning. Yiannis made it to the Eye in a matter of minutes and instituted all the processes to override the codes installed by Moussa.

Yiannis had brought enough mermaid muscle that when asked to leave, the Senegalese employees flew out the doors of the casino, leaving Yiannis to run the show.

Similar actions happened simultaneously at both the Amalfi club and the one in Athens. Everything had been meticulously synchronized.

Moussa was en route to Argentina for a negotiation when he got the news that Yiannis had taken over. Moussa spent the rest of the day making travel arrangements for his people to get back to Dakar.

Stemming off a panic attack with a new prescription of antianxiety meds, this was one of the million times Moussa missed Oumar. Oumar would have had a plan, would have known what to do, would have been able to talk Moussa off any ledge. As of late, Queen Awa had been tied up in global politics, leaving Moussa in charge of the monied operations. Now he realized he was failing, at least in the short term.

Feeling despondent, he dialed his mother.

"*Maman*, we have a problem. I think we need to meet in Dakar and regroup."

47

February 1996

"I have not been hiding from you, Florent," Gia said, pressing the button for her floor, and turning the key to allow her access to it.

"No?" His stomach was churning, with nerves, with anger. "Then why does it feel that you have been? I've been *everywhere* looking for you."

"*Amore*," she sighed, "I am a grown up woman, you know. I have a company to run. I do not have time to play hide and seek with teenagers."

Rage shot through him like lightning.

The doors parted, and Gia stepped out of the elevator.

He followed.

She calmly opened the door to her suite, and Florent slipped in behind her. She could tell from how red he was in the face that he was furious with her. In fact, he probably wanted to kill her. Gia couldn't help but scoff at the idea. He didn't scare her one bit.

"Pour us two glasses of bourbon while I change," she said, hanging her coat on a hook.

"I don't think I will," he hissed.

She clicked her tongue against her teeth and turned heel, heading to the wet bar. Gia passed him a drink and invited him into the living room. The suite's large windows overlooked the snow-capped hills. She clicked a switch on the wall, and the gas fireplace ignited.

Florent seethed. "You think you are so charming and sexy, don't you?"

She peered at him over the rim of her glass—and smirked knowingly.

"You are here, are you not?" she quipped. "It seems that I am sexy enough for you to have been chasing me around the world. So, perhaps you are the expert on that matter."

"It's not like you have a magic pussy, Gia. I... I have been with other... other women... and you're nothing special."

She couldn't help but laugh at him. He looked like a little boy throwing a fit over not having a big enough scoop on his ice cream cone.

She nuzzled into the leather couch in front of the fire.

"Florent, what is it that you want from me?"

He threw his glass on the stone floor.

As it smashed, Gia felt transported for a moment to the night that Pierre died. She remembered Pierre's glass breaking on the wall, shattering into a million glittery pieces, moments prior to his body breaking apart after his fall. She shook her head to wrestle herself free from the past.

Then she glanced up to see that Florent was standing over her. The reflection of the fire danced in his animal eyes.

He lurched toward her.

48

December 13th

Harper forced a thoroughly convincing smile as she cradled her niece. After days of not being administered the hormone, Serena's golden tail was back in all its shining glory. Harper wasn't sure whether to cover it in the winter weather, so she'd dressed Serena in a cashmere turtleneck and a matching beret.

Serena was gurgling and happy under the bright lights of the hotel ballroom where Goldie had set up the latest press conference.

Harper tapped on the mic to check the sound and began.

"Thank you all for joining me this afternoon. The public's outpouring of support has been really moving. This is a strange time, but I'm really happy to announce that today the New York Family Court made the right decision for my niece, Serena, and awarded me temporary custody."

Outside the doors to the ballroom the crowd that had gathered broke out into riotous cheers.

"I'll take a few questions now." She pointed at a familiar face in the press pool. "Matt, go."

"Is it true that the Westchester County Police served a search warrant to your parents' legal team to check out their home?"

"Matt, you know better than to ask me that, right? I can't comment on criminal investigations. Furthermore, I'm only in contact with my parents through our legal teams."

"Follow up?" Matt shouted.

"Sure."

"In the wake of the mounting criminal case against Gia Acquaviva and your parents, will you seek permanent custody?"

"Let's cross that bridge when we come to it." Harper looked further to the back, spotting Ashely Mason. To fuck with her, she pointed in Ashley's direction before calling out the name of another reporter.

"Will you allow Serena to see her mother?"

"I'll do what the court recommends. Next, you."

Before the reporter could ask anything, Ashley Mason wrestled away a microphone. "Harper, how does it feel to betray your parents? How exactly do you plan to care for a baby—a merbaby no less—when you've never even been around children? Are your actions out of spite, or are the online rumors true... and you've been paid off by Gia Acquaviva?"

"I'm not scared of you, Ash. And I'm not scared of my mom and dad. If they did what Gia's saying they did, they deserve whatever comes next."

With that, Harper walked behind a LION step and repeat and laid Serena in a baby carriage.

"Shit," she huffed, "here we go, Serena. Let me get you home."

Cam, you asshole, of course you had to go and knock up a mermaid and leave me to deal with this shit squall. Help me out here, bro. Pull some strings up there for me. Ashley's right about one thing. I have no idea what I'm doing.

49

February 1996

Florent's hands were around Gia's throat, squeezing hard. Beneath the skin of her forearms, her gills ruffled, awakening.

She kicked his legs out from under him, and he fell to the floor, losing his grip on her neck. Once on the ground, he crumpled into a ball and wailed. Her gills were fully out now, but how could she attack him? He looked so small and so sad. There would be no thrill in that kind of strike—nothing about a pathetic victim turned her on. She took several deep breaths to calm herself and stroked her arms until the gills once again took their place below her muscles.

"Get up," she commanded.

Florent just laid there, sobbing.

She sunk back into the couch and watched him. His body shivered.

"I cannot give you what you want, Florent."

"What?" he screeched, breath ragged.

"Do you want me to say that I am sorry for what happened to your father?"

He lifted his head to look in her direction.

"Florent," she leaned forward, locking her eyes on his, "I am not sorry. I do not care. I have barely given Pierre a moment's thought since that day. He is gone. It does not help you or your father to carry on in this manner."

"What the fuck, Gia. What's wrong with you?"

She stared at the fire and didn't answer.

"No matter what I do, or who I'm with, I never stop thinking of you, Gia. Can you honestly tell me that you don't feel the same?"

"Love is not a fairytale, Florent. I am not a princess, *amore.*"

As she observed Florent's tear-streaked face, she reflected back on her time with Pierre. After all, Florent and his father looked very much alike, and she saw so many of Pierre's expressions play out on Florent's face.

On the whole, Pierre had been tiresome. A sweet man, but a bore. His money had been helpful for Gia, though. And Florent? He had been much more fun than his father. She almost felt proud of herself for bringing a man to his knees like this, but she also felt disgusted by Florent's show of emotion.

His total vulnerability, on the other hand, meant that she had him in her palm if that's where she wanted him. She tilted her head, considering her options. She wasn't finished toying with Serge yet, so his date with death was months down the line. In that moment, Gia realized that she had an opportunity in front of her.

Of course, she couldn't slit Florent's throat right here in her hotel room. That would be a mess, and she wasn't in the mood to clean up a mess.

"Florent, today has been rather a lot for you. I think you should go."

He hung his head.

"But," Gia said, her words dangling in the air like icicles, "I would like to see you again."

"Really?" he asked, his voice hoarse, but with a ray of hope shining through.

"Tomorrow is the full moon. I have always wanted to skate on a frozen lake during a full moon. Will you join me?"

50

December 14th

Anger melted through Gia like molten glass in a Murano factory. She glared at each face on the Zoom call: Queen Awa, Prince Moussa, President João, Prime Minister Pablo del Rio Dulce, as well as a delegate from the Arctic Circle. She then turned her burning scorn to *La Nonna*.

"*Abbastanza*!" she growled. "*Non più*! If you do not understand me, I am saying NO MORE. I have been patient. I have played everyone else's moves for months now, and where am I? My baby has been stolen by my sociopathic sister-in-law. My business is in ruins like the Colosseum. The police are investigating me for murder!"

Silence permeated the room and online.

"Today the game changes. From now on we play by my rules. Understood?"

Queen Awa cleared her throat. "Are you finished with your rant?"

"*Excuse me*?" Gia seethed.

"I am of half a mind to tell you to go fuck yourself. Do not ever speak to me in this way again. I am a Queen, and you will treat me with respect. Not to mention I have been toiling away trying to save your ass, save your little *pina colada* empire... and moving sea and clay to bring together the very people on this call today. Now, apologize and let's start over with a renewed attitude, shall we?"

La Nonna sucked her lips in and bit them to keep from exploding into laughter. She was both amused and jealous of the way Queen Awa put Gia in her place.

Long overdue, she thought.

Gia let out a dry croak "Ah—"

"No, no, sweet thing. The next words I want to hear out of your mouth are, 'I am very sorry.' Otherwise this call is over."

Gia swallowed and straightened her back. She opened her mouth to spew more venom, but closed it quickly and shook her head. "Sincere apologies."

Queen Awa narrowed her eyes, "That's a start. Continue."

"When I was still living in Venice, I discovered that Harper had placed surveillance in my *palazzo*." Gia turned to face *La Nonna*. "You suggested that we 'return the favor,' and I would like to know... *if you do not mind...* whether these cameras are still active and being monitored?"

"*Bene*, of course," *La Nonna* replied, smirking.

"Excellent. What I would like very much to do is to remove my daughter from Harper's apartment and leave the land of Big Macs and super soda. Yes?"

"Happily, *angioletta*."

"Perfect. And I would also love to ask, Your Majesty, Queen Awa, whether I might be accepted as a guest in the Coral Tower?"

"Gia," Queen Awa lowered her head with equanimity, "you are always welcome in Senegal."

"Thank you. When I arrive with my daughter, *perhaps*, Prince Moussa, we can begin to plan how we might regain control of my empire... and expand yours."

"*Mais, oui*," he giggled.

"*Finalmente*," Gia turned her attention to the other Pan-Atargatic leaders on the call, "I understand that because of my decisions, the terrain has forever shifted both above ground and on the ocean floor.

I do not know you well, but I would like for you to understand something important about me. When someone strikes me, I strike back twice as strong. Greece and California have certain weaknesses that I feel we may be able to exploit."

President João shrugged his shoulders. "We could be persuaded to explore this course of action."

"It appears we are in agreement," Gia said, folding her hands on the table. "Then we should continue the conversation. I have a few ideas in mind."

51

December 17th

The Westchester Police rolled up, sirens blazing around five o'clock in the afternoon.

The police chief wanted footage for the evening news.

The Langleys' attorneys had spent the day negotiating, and this was the best the police would settle for: gates open at Langley Manor, Royce and Bronwyn surrendering with no fuss, no cuffs, and Chief escorting them into a black Suburban.

And so it was.

At the appointed hour, the arrest ceremony took place as planned. What had not been planned—or disclosed to the Langleys' attorneys—was that several additional parties were present at the Westchester Police Station.

The Commissioner of the NYPD and several Feds.

Gia's exposing the Langleys had been the best news possible for multiple arms of the state and federal authorities. This case had the potential to blow the doors off Royce and Bronwyn's entire operation. Years of case files that had previously led nowhere had been revived and reopened with fervor in the past week.

Tax evasion? Maybe. Insider trading? Most likely. Bribery. Hell yeah, tons of that.

In short, the Langleys' hubris in thinking they could best Gia had completely and utterly fucked them.

* * *

WHEN GIA HEARD the news about Royce and Bronwyn's arrest, she was puzzled as to why she had not also been arrested. The truth was that while Gia was a juicy dish, the authorities were gorging themselves on Langley meat first.

Furthermore, with her intense popularity nationally, the police and the Feds knew they would face a tsunami of outrage, and possible protests, the moment they moved on Gia.

They figured there was plenty of time to deal with her later.

Gia, however, had other plans.

La Nonna's team of goons idled on standby, ready to break into Harper's place at a moment's notice. All they had to do was wait for the right time to present itself.

In the meantime, Gia's role was to behave normally. Besides, she had something important to do: say goodbye to Riley.

Gia turned up in the West Village unexpectedly, security team in tow.

The doorman buzzed the crew up, and Riley opened her door. "This is a surprise," she said to Gia, eyes full of mischief. "I see you've brought the cavalry. Guys, come in and grab some chairs."

Riley held the door open as the men hauled her expensive dining room chairs into the hallway.

"How did your movie shoot go? Do you wear a cape and turn cartwheels?" Gia asked, propping herself against the kitchen island.

"Shut up," Riley grabbed Gia's shoulders and pulled her in, kissing her deeply. "I missed you, you bitch. Atlanta sucks. I have to go back on Sunday. Wanna come?"

Gia cocked her head to the side. "To what? To sit in your trailer and fetch you water?"

"Sometimes you are far less charming than you think you are."

Gia winced.

"Can't take a hit, can you, Gia? But you sure like to punch, don't you?" Riley reached into the fridge and pulled out a bottle of white wine. "I'm not supposed to drink this right now, but I have a feeling you're going to tell me bad news."

Gia pushed her hair out of her face and crossed the kitchen, headed to the sofa. "Why do you think this?"

Riley let out a breathy laugh as she poured two glasses. Then she met Gia on the other side of the apartment.

After taking a few big sips from her glass, Riley clicked her tongue and focused on Gia. "Listen, I really like you."

Gia sat in silence.

"Um... Gia? I was kind of expecting you to say you like me, too."

"What is this about, Riley?"

"My agent... um... he's telling me that he wants me to cool it with you for a while. The whole murder thing... he says it's not playing well with the studio execs." She paused for a moment to laugh. "Fair enough, right? They think it's a time bomb."

"*Bene*, so—"

"But I don't really care, to be honest. I've never met anyone like you, Gia. I've never met... well... anyone like *me*."

"Anyone like you?"

"Come on, don't be coy with me. You're a little killer. You've got bloodlust. You're fucking Medieval."

Gia found she'd stopped breathing for a moment.

"I think we're perfect for each other. I would cut off a piece of you and put it in a locket if you'd let me."

Gia's heartbeat thumped, and she felt... what was the feeling, exactly? She'd never really had it—not for a person anyway. Was it fear? No, not precisely. Gia had experienced real terror in her time with Q, and what she felt now was something else.

"Riley..." Gia's words got caught in her throat.

"Gia, I want to watch you kill someone. I'm *aching* for it. Do you understand how good it feels to admit that?"

She did, indeed. As much as she felt unsettled and disturbed by what Riley was expressing, Gia also found herself drawn in.

"All I'm saying," Riley rattled on, "is that I'm all in. I want to know how you feel."

"I—"

"Don't break my heart. I'm serious."

"Are you threatening me?"

"Do you *really* think I'd threaten you after what I saw you do to that mafia guy?"

Gia's mouth was going dry. She felt confused, and the room was turning all wobbly. For a second, she panicked.

Did Riley put something in my drink?

Gia blinked a few times and her surroundings came back into focus.

"So?" Riley needled. "What is it? How do you feel?"

"Do you want the truth?"

"Yeah!"

"I... I think I might be falling in love with you, Riley."

52

February 1996

Louisa spotted Florent in the lobby and rushed over. "Where have you been?" she shouted. "We have been looking for you everywhere!" Then she noticed how red and splotchy his face was. "What has happened? What is wrong, *amore*?"

Amore. The word struck a blow against his chest, and it made his heart ache. Louisa really was such a poor placeholder for Gia. Now that the genuine article had finally reappeared in his life, Louisa felt silly and superfluous.

"I'm fine," he snapped. "Let's go back to the chalet."

But he couldn't wait to rid himself of her.

* * *

FLORENT GOT good and drunk in the evening. He was even more quiet than normal, and not at all charming. Rather than spend another painful moment with him, Louisa excused herself and went up to their room.

The moon rose and lit up the snowy hills like a silver sun. He pulled on his puffy white ski jacket, topped his head with a cap, and practically rolled out the door, heavy as a snowman.

He trudged through the paths, up stairs, and over a small mountain, before arriving at the *rendezvous* point.

Gia crouched at the edge of the frozen lake, lacing up a pair of ice skates. She wore a black jumpsuit and leather gloves.

"Come to me," she curled her finger, beckoning him.

Florent no longer felt raw as he had in the afternoon. The booze had buffed the edges, buoyed him. He floated over to her.

When he approached her, he found Gia pouting. "Everything was a bit too hot earlier. I did not realize you had such strong feelings for me."

With her words, Florent felt as though he had become a wishing well, one that Gia carelessly dipped her fingers in, swirling them about. The sensation was both pleasant and disturbing.

"Help me up." She held her hand out, and he took it. She wobbled and fell into his arms. Her head landed over his shoulder, and she whispered, "*Scussi*." Her breath tickled his earlobe, and he tilted his head down, closing his eyes. He hoped that the moment would stretch on forever. He would have gladly frozen in place and become a statue.

She pulled back from him, and their gaze met.

For the first time he saw sadness in her eyes. He felt a tug inside, like there was a string running from his heart to her body.

His mind flashed back to the time at La Perle Noire, when he'd slipped his fingers between her legs. He'd been in such control then. He had not imagined that he would have ended up feeling like a tin can, tied to her car, driven around Europe at high speeds.

He was hers whether she wanted him or not.

He couldn't take his eyes off her.

And then she arched forward and kissed him. Her lips burned hot against his. She spread them, and his tongue entered her mouth, and he groaned, pulling her closer.

He couldn't remember the number of times he'd acted out this same kiss with Louisa. But this was... more than he could have imagined. She tasted better than he remembered.

Her kisses were all over him. She ran her hands down his chest and over his hips, landing on the zipper of his pants. Down it went, and then... in he went, into her leather-clad hand. She tickled him, tracing her finger around the head of his cock.

He held his breath.

Gia bent to her knees and took him in her mouth. He felt unsteady on his feet, and so she tugged him down onto the ice with her, barely taking her mouth off of him.

She took her time sucking him off, stopping every time that she thought he might come, looking up at him with narrowed eyes and a breathy laugh.

He endured this wonderful torture for as long as he could, and when she felt his heart begin to beat in his cock, she took her mouth off of him and watched as he came onto his jacket and the ice below.

She slid her face up to his.

"Did you like that?" she asked.

He couldn't manage any words, so he just nodded very slowly.

"I loved that," she said.

Then, rather nonchalantly, she embraced his face before shoving her right sleeve up to her elbow.

He saw something strange happen then. Maybe it was a trick of the light. Something on her arm seemed to reflect the moonlight.

But Florent could not ponder further—it all happened so fast.

The shimmer on her forearm, and then... then the fast movement as she raised her arm and brought it down onto his neck.

He didn't even have time to make a sound before he felt a sharp blade cut into the skin below the left side of his chin. It traveled diagonally, bouncing over his Adam's apple, and then to the base of his neck on the right.

His mouth shook.

He hadn't focused his eyes on anything until he saw the big, flat moon hovering over him, and then Gia's head leaning into it. The moon looked like a crown behind her, as if she was a religious icon, an angel.

Her eyes, though... her eyes were a demon's. Black and focused, dancing with delight.

Florent's blood seeped out from him, pooling under his neck. It spread out on the ice like spilled cherry sauce.

In the distance, from the pathway he'd traveled to get to the lake, someone laughed. No, more than one person, a few people. Their voices traveled fast and far.

Florent tried to call out to them, but he found he was unable to scream.

The pleasure in Gia's eyes turned quickly into panic. She shoved away from him, slipping across the ice. She grabbed her shoes, holding them to her chest—and then used a solid amount of adrenaline to pull herself up. She strode across the lake in thick lines.

She was fast, faster than she imagined she could be.

Fast enough, though? She hoped so.

The lake was wide, but it curved around a hillside.

She barely breathed until she glided out of sight.

At the edge of the lake, she tore off her gloves and tucked them into her breasts. Then she struggled with her shoelaces, trying to rip the skates off. She ended up tossing each of them as far as she could.

God, how she wished she could dive into that icy lake and hide out at the bottom. Instead, she ran through the snow with no shoes. Her socks were soaked through.

But Serge's house was nearby. Just up the hill.

She eyed the chalet and the warm puff of smoke snaking from the chimney.

And she ran.

53

December 19th

Harper's mobile phone buzzed. A photo of a two-headed dragon appeared. The name on the caller ID was Marlee Taylor.

"Marlee?"

"This is Marlee's assistant, I'll put you through."

Can you not?

"Sounds good," Harper replied to the assistant. She frowned deep down to her core as she waited on the line.

"Harpie!" Marlee's voice shone like a fake sun.

Harper grimaced. "How can I help you Marlee?"

"We need you to come in."

"To the OTN office?" Harper asked, confused.

"No, Harper, to the Board. We want you to step in while your father's... out."

"Ahhh... Marlee, you know I'm with Goldie now."

"Let me talk to Goldie. I'm sure we can work something out. We'll buy you out of your contract with him."

"Marlee, this is not really a convenient time for me to reboot my relationship with OTN."

"Harper, we need you. What's it going to take to get you over here?"

"I don't think you understand. I'm not interested."

"Hmm. Well, that is really unfortunate."

"It was nice—"

"Harper, your apartment... it's owned by the network, right?"

"What?"

"And you own... mmm... not an insignificant percentage of stock in the company."

"Right..."

Marlee sucked her teeth, "It would be *terrible* if the stock price tanked. You know, Royce's assets are really entangled with the company's. So, it would be a real *shame* if we were to cooperate with the authorities to the full extent that we could. You'd really lose a lot. Maybe... *everything*."

Harper exhaled and practically grunted the next words. "Send me a calendar invite."

"No need, Harper. We're all here. We'd like you to come in *now*."

"I can't do that, Marlee. I don't know if you've been watching the news, but I'm playing mother hen to my niece at the moment."

"No worries. We're sending a sitter now, and a car to pick you up."

* * *

HARPER LEFT her building with her bodyguard in tow, stopping by the on-duty doorman and porter on her way out.

"Guys, I'm leaving the baby with a sitter. Please keep an eye on things for me."

The doorman tilted his uniform's cap to her, "You got it, ma'am."

"Thanks."

Moments later the two men were back to arguing over their rival basketball teams. They didn't even register the front doors of the building opening, nor did they notice what was happening as they bantered.

Three men entered the lobby, their faces covered in pantyhose.

Two of them raised tasers and zapped the porter and doorman.

The thugs whipped out the "Be Right Back" sign from inside the lobby desk and dragged the men into the elevator with them, traveling with them right up to Harper's door. After zip ties and gags were applied, the third man popped the lock on the front door, and they barrelled in.

The babysitter shrieked and ran toward the bathroom, but she was tazed as well and collapsed in the middle of the living room.

The men headed to the guest room and gently picked up Serena, smuggling her in her carseat to a getaway vehicle that waited in the basement parking lot.

The whole thing took less than five minutes.

They met Gia on 37th street, where the Port Authority buses normally parked. Gia stepped out of one car, as the guys exited theirs. One man handed the baby off to Gia, and she entered an unmarked bread truck that sped off, passing through the Holland Tunnel on the way to an airfield in deep Jersey, where Gia's plane was waiting.

Gia strapped Serena into a baby holster and wrapped her arms around her child, stroking Serena's blonde curls and inhaling her baby scent. The feeling of completeness almost brought her to tears.

"I cannot believe I ever doubted my love for you, my baby. My sweet, sweet baby. Mamma has you now, and you will be safe. Tonight we fly to Senegal, and tomorrow, you will meet a whole colony of mermaids just like you."

54

December 19th

Queen Zale had never set foot on a plane, much less a private one headed from the Mediterranean directly to Dakar. Queen Karen had hitched a ride with her sons on their jet share to pick up her very, very old friend.

They were joined by an intimate group of Zale's generals.

When the plane landed, they boarded a speedboat, which took them far enough out to sea, close enough to the Coral Tower. The small army disrobed and dove into the cold waves of the Atlantic Ocean.

The boat turned immediately around to head back to shore, as the captain had been instructed. There, he docked the boat, lifted it up, and secured it with extra attention.

Underwater, Queens Zale and Karen swam around each other in circles, dovetailing one another over and over. They chanted an ancient prayer, and soon they spun faster as the water gathered around them. They created a thin cyclone that stretched from the seafloor to the surface of the water.

Their bodies became illuminated, and the sounds radiating off of the queens were hellishly loud, mimicking the screams of a million thrashing souls.

They stretched their bodies out, pressing away from the current and cast the twister through the water. The generals helped guide the flow of the path of the storm, ensuring it hit its target.

The typhoon picked up everything in its wake: sand, sea creatures, and plant life… and when it neared the Coral Tower, it claimed the graves of the dead. Oumar's gravestone lifted, and his bones scattered in the current. The grave marker bounced frantically, like a penny released from a pair of jeans in the wash, and then innocently, it crashed through the glass window on the seventeenth floor of the Tower with a violent thud.

Projectiles sprayed through the Coral Tower's glass structure—a meteor shower of sea magic.

Water crashed upon the floors soaking everything in its path before shattering every surface under the weight of its touch.

The lights went out.

Queen Awa and her wife, alone in their suite, were swept away by the brutal tide. Moussa was thrown out to sea.

* * *

As Gia's plane descended into Dakar, she surveyed the devastation wrought by the attack. The underwater typhoon had caused incredibly destructive flooding along the coast of the city. Some beaches were washed away entirely, leaving only sharp and broken cliffs. Hundreds of dead merfolk had washed ashore, as did sea life of every ilk.

It was days before she learned that the disaster had been caused by her own kind.

EPILOGUE

The sun was setting in Paris. Florent and Gia's little girls played with dolls together on the living room rug.

Florent laid his head on Gia's shoulder. She stroked his hair, and then ran two fingers down his cheek, below his chin. He held his breath as she traced the outline of his mangled scar. Gia's heart beat faster as she remembered how he'd gotten it.

Florent felt Gia's hair fall on his face as she leaned closer to him.

"I want you," she whispered into his ear.

"*Tsk Tsk,*" he grinned. "It's the scar every time. You are so predictable, Gia."

She eyed him with a tiger's gaze.

He bit his lip. "Let me put the girls to bed."

When he left the room, her phone lit up with a notification, a text.

It was from Riley.

The text read, *I'm coming to Paris,* and it was followed by a smiling purple devil emoji.

Gia quickly deleted the message and tucked her phone into her purse before meeting Pierre in their bedroom.

IF YOU LOVED THIS...

Love this book? Leave a review!

Dying to know what's next for Gia?
Pre-order the next book in the series today!

WANT MORE FROM ME RIGHT NOW?
Simply scan the QR code below and join my Insider Circle.

SCAN ME

ALSO BY JINCEY LUMPKIN

Mermaid of Venice (Book 1)

Mermaid of Sicily (Book 2)

Mermaid of Paris (Book 4, coming May 2022)

Mermaid of St. Moritz (Book 5, coming June 2022)

Mermaid of Monte Carlo (Book 6, coming August 2022)

Sirena de Venecia (*Mermaid of Venice*, Spanish language version)

Made in the USA
Monee, IL
15 February 2022

660b7886-69a6-487d-94da-d3931c9ee882R01